"When you live on the edge of a cursed for...
– Sarah

Systema Paradoxa

Accounts of cryptozoological import

Volume 05
Devil in the Green
A Tale of the Montauk Monster

As accounted by James Chambers

NeoParadoxa
Pennsville, NJ
2021

PUBLISHED BY
NeoParadoxa
A division of eSpec Books
PO Box 242
Pennsville, NJ 08070
www.especbooks.com

Copyright © 2021 James Chambers

ISBN: 978-1-949691-59-7
ISBN (ebook): 978-1-949691-58-0

Interior Design: Danielle McPhail
www.sidhenadaire.com

Cover Art: Jason Whitley
Cover Design: Mike and Danielle McPhail, McP Digital Graphics
Interior Illustration: Jason Whitley

Copyediting: Greg Schauer and John L. French

DEDICATION

FOR MY MOM

FOREWORD

*The following account tells an incredible and shocking story — but it is not
my own.*

*I have carefully reconstructed and assembled this narrative from notes and
recordings given me by a man I know as Benjamin Keep and presented it, as
much as possible, in Mr. Keep's own voice, in many places weaving into the text
extracts and quotes from his notes and journals. For reasons I'm not at liberty
to divulge, Mr. Keep prefers to share what he learned during the occurrences of
this tale at arm's length from the public. You can imagine the scrutiny and
backlash that might follow such claims that the events described here are true
and occurred exactly as you shall read them — and this is Mr. Keep's contention.*

*By sharing this record, he hopes to enrich and enlighten the world, but he
does not wish to be dogged by questions, or skeptics, or opportunists, by proof-
seekers, or critics, or other explorers into mystery. For the latter, he asks that if
you take anything of importance from this tale, it be the reminder that those
who sojourn into the twilight world where mysteries live must forge their own
path. Think for yourself, always. Take no one at their word, nothing at face
value. Seek out your own evidence. Seek the truth. Never lose sight of the big
picture and the context in which we exist, in which the universe exists. And
understand that facts can be made to serve lies, used to dress up deceptions in
appealing fashions, and as easily as they may expose the truth, they may also
bury it. Should anyone reading this undertake to locate Mr. Keep, you will not
find him by that name. Nor will you find any of the others mentioned in this
narrative by the names used here.*

*Although I met with Mr. Keep several times while writing this document,
he exerted no influence over what I chose to include or exclude or how I
characterized him and his companions. I assume he approved of or, at least,
found my depictions accurate enough to satisfy his standards, which I found
quite high. I have scrupulously refrained from allowing my own opinions and*

insights to seep into this narrative. Mr. Keep gave me this tale to tell, but the experiences, questions, and conclusions remain his alone. Even in this foreword, I resist temptations to offer my own perspectives and feelings on what I've written here, and if anyone who reads this should seek me out, I will not discuss them. I know nothing more of the story than what is contained here and decline in advance to respond to questions I cannot possibly answer.

I ask no one to believe the events and phenomena recounted here. That choice is yours. If you should find the story incredible and fantastic beyond credulity, then I hope, at least, you find it entertaining. I also hope, in some fashion, it opens your eyes to those parts of the world — those truths — forever nearby and yet perpetually hidden in shadow.

— James Chambers
Northport, NY

CHAPTER ONE

I never intended to hunt monsters.

That strange summer that found me combing Long Island's south shore beaches and wandering through its nearby Pine Barrens forever changed my life. The resolution to every mystery I encountered during those hot and humid months only led to greater enigmas, each one branching, hydra-like, when I believed it resolved, sprouting new lines of investigation that led me farther from the certainty of the ordinary world into one overshadowed by phenomena few people ever encounter.

The events of that summer provided me a glimpse at the inner workings of the universe and awakened in me a deep dread and understanding of humanity's cosmic insignificance, although with too little information to make any sense of it. Perhaps there is no sense to it. Perhaps chaos defines all existence, a string of random biological, chemical, and physical actions and reactions. Atoms and molecules colliding, binding, reinventing their substance. The ceaseless transformation of energy. Mistakes of awareness. Sentience nothing more than a glitch in space and time. I don't believe these things, but if existence does possess purpose, it reaches far beyond mere human experience and comprehension.

All of this, I realize, sounds like something out of a century-old pulp magazine or the liner notes for some Sixties prog-rock album, but to this day, I still grapple with how to describe my experiences. I struggle to explain, even to myself, how opening a shoebox full of old bones knocked my entire world off its axis.

I wonder if Dr. Annetta Maikels, who brought me to that time and place, suspected what her investigation into an animal carcass more than a decade old might uncover. Did she seek to open Pandora's box?

Or did she, as she explained when we first met, mean only to debunk a local legend?

A quirk of chance brought Annetta to my door late that June. Ethan Scapetti, a college friend of mine and a reporter for a Long Island daily newspaper, introduced us after he broke his leg and four ribs in a car crash. Two days before his appointment to cover Annetta's viewing of the remains of the so-called Montauk Monster, a black sedan side-swiped his car off the road into a telephone pole, a hit-and-run accident. I had freelanced for his paper, shooting photo features of local events for its website. Ethan hoped to throw the work my way, knowing I sorely needed it and hoping I'd take the assignment more seriously than any of the jaded staff reporters who might cover it for him.

After wishing him a speedy recovery, I brushed up on the lore of the Montauk Monster, finding blessed little to learn. The infamous photo from the 2008 sighting of its carcass at Ditch Plains Beach, Montauk looked to me exactly as most experts described it: the remains of a small dog or raccoon, grotesquely distorted by decomposition and several days floating in salt water. The remains vanished soon after the sighting, reportedly removed by a local resident who then buried them on their property or stored them in a garage. They were never seen again. Thanks to a Gawker.com headline, the picture went viral and sparked the imaginations of millions around the world.

The group of young women who snapped the photo offered little information. After first embracing the limelight, they later shied away from it and the Montauk Monster altogether.

That single image, however, birthed an unforgettable beast. Reports of similar creatures followed from around the world, as close as Staten Island and as far away as Asia. None of them offered proof of anything other than that a few days of ocean exposure could dramatically alter the appearance of a small, dead mammal. Still, something in that first photo, in the deformed body and more so in the sharp, unnatural lines of its muzzle leading to a sort of beak nagged at me enough that I couldn't firmly close the door on the possibility of another explanation. That odd head and beak conjured memories of illustrations in childhood books about prehistoric giant mammals, so out of place in 2008 that I understood why it fascinated many who saw it. More than a decade later, a second Ditch Plains sighting reignited interest in the so-called Montauk Monster.

A couple walking the beach discovered the second carcass, which resembled the original creature in almost every detail, except that it retained a bit more of its fur, bleached gray by sun and salt water. They shot a photo with a composition similar to the 2008 image, but it failed to achieve the same viral popularity. With all the grim, depressing news in the world that year, perhaps no one had the heart for monster stories. But for those already interested in Monty, as Annetta liked to call the thing, it offered hope of validation, opening a new chapter in the legend. More importantly, it inspired Annetta, a biology and zoology professor at King's College in Brooklyn, to use her summer break to indulge her infatuation with cryptozoology and investigate an enticing lead. For that, I am forever grateful—because it brought her to my door.

CHAPTER TWO

Annetta arrived at my house in Hicksville early on a Saturday morning.

Her stature and confidence intimidated me from the moment I saw her. Close to six feet tall, she almost matched my own height. She wore hiking boots and khaki shorts, a green T-shirt under a light, short-sleeved jacket loaded with pockets, and a satchel slung across her torso. With dark, brown skin and close-cut hair, she looked smart, adventurous, and official. The sight of her immediately altered my impression of the assignment, and I regretted answering the door in faded college sweatpants and an old *Adventure Time* T-shirt.

"Benjamin Keep?" she said.

"That's me." I invited her in for a cup of coffee while I changed clothes and gathered my camera, a high-quality digital SLR that had set me back several months' worth of student-loan payments, and soon we hit the road. Annetta drove a Prius that seemed too small to contain her. She refused to share with me the address of our destination.

"I promised I'd keep it a secret," she said, and when I pointed out that I'd learn it when we got there, she grinned and said, "Maybe."

We merged into highway traffic and sped east along the Long Island Expressway, another furious insect joining the frantic scurry along the asphalt ant trail.

"What do you know about cryptozoology?" Annetta asked me.

"What the average person knows from watching Bigfoot documentaries and looking at pictures of the Loch Ness Monster online," I told her. "But I've read up on the Montauk Monster."

"Yeah? So, tell me what you know about Monty."

I ran down what I'd learned from my research.

She nodded. "Well done, Ben, and yeah, I've heard all the explanations for why Monty isn't a cryptid. Publicity stunt, dead raccoon, latex hoax. Maybe one of them is right—but maybe none of them are."

"You hope to prove it one way or the other?" I slid a notebook and pen from my camera case. "This is for the record, by the way."

"Nope, not looking to prove anything. Only theories require proof, and I have no theory yet. But I don't like the other theories. I'm gathering evidence to form my own theory."

"How did you learn the location of the remains, and what makes you believe they're authentic?"

"The owner called me out of the blue. Said she heard about my interest from mutual acquaintances. But I don't believe anything yet. I mostly expect at the end of this trip out to the ass-end of Long Island we're going to wind up looking at a collection of squirrel bones. If we're lucky, they'll be dressed up to look like something weird, and we'll be entertained."

"Like the Feejee Mermaid."

"Exactly. PT Barnum at his finest. Gold star for you. If we're very, very lucky, though, they'll turn out to be something special."

"The remains of the 2008 creature?"

"Wouldn't that be nice?"

I agreed it would, then shifted gears. "What attracted you to cryptozoology?"

Annetta laughed. "Now there's a long story."

"We've got a long drive."

The nomadic tribes of summer thickened and forced us to slow down, to fall into place with the great migration of beach-seekers, wine-tasters, and antique-hunters fleeing stifling New York City and suburban boredom for Long Island's once-pastoral East End. As a native Long Islander, I made a point of avoiding Montauk, the Hamptons, and the transplanted city social scene that flooded the Island every summer. Upper-East- and West-Siders, for whom most of the Island counted as the local flyover country, looked down their noses at we suburbanites. The "bridge-and-tunnel" crowd, they called us, but their snobbery never hindered their annual invasion of the South Fork from Memorial Day to Labor Day.

Annetta frowned at the mass of surrounding cars, but as the sunlight warmed my face and I eyed the clear blue sky, it surprised me traffic moved anything above an absolute crawl on such a near-perfect summer day.

"Damn this traffic. We need to be there before noon. The owner was insistent about that. I don't want to roll up at 12:05 and have a door slammed in our faces."

The dashboard clock read 10:12. "We'll make it. Might cut it close, but this traffic's got to thin out sometime. Tell me your story and take your mind off all this."

After a sigh, Annetta said, "Okay, you ever hear stories about the alligators in the sewers?"

"Where? In the City?"

"Right. People bring home baby alligators as pets from trips to Florida or Georgia or wherever. Their kids love them for a few weeks, then get bored and forget about them. The baby gators grow a little too big, flash some teeth, and then suddenly, a light bulb goes on in Mom or Dad's head. This thing will get huge and need food. They don't want to deal with it, and their kids hardly remember they have it. So, one night while everyone's asleep or some afternoon while the kids are at school, they flush the poor gator down the toilet, good riddance."

"Yeah, I know this one. There's an old movie about it. The gator survives its toilet ride, winds up in the sewer, where it grows to full size, and roams around under the city, chowing down on sewer workers. It's a classic urban legend."

A tractor-trailer, finding a miraculous opening amongst the cars, flew by us, shuddering Annetta's Prius with its backdraft. To either side of the road sprawled the Pine Barrens, dark and unkempt, one of the last great spaces of Long Island yet to face bulldozers and conversion into strip malls and townhome developments. Protected, for now, it persisted under development rumors that circled like sharks. Proposals for a 600-acre golf course, a casino, eco-housing, and even an adventure park had all tested the strength of the law protecting more than 100,000 acres of wilderness. Surrounded by it, Annetta's story sounded like a campfire tale, and a shiver ran through me.

"My grandmother told me about the alligators when I was in second grade," Annetta said. "Scared me silly. I refused to ride the subway for a month after that. My mother was furious with her because I made us walk everywhere or take the bus. One time we even took a cab because I cried so hard when she tried to carry me down the stairs at Jay Street Station. Eventually, my fear gave way to other worries, schoolwork, who was coming to my birthday party, other kid stuff. My mom promised me a Snickers if I took the subway again. She figured I'd see there wasn't anything to be afraid of, and we could get back to normal. My first time back, though, wouldn't you know it? I saw an alligator down there."

"Wait, seriously?"

"Seriously, yes, but not really. My mother liked to board at the front of the train. We always waited near the end of the platform, with a view of the tunnel, and I saw all sorts of stuff on the tracks. Cockroaches. Rats. Litter. And that one time, in the darkness where the rails curved out of sight into the gloom, I saw something big and frightening with a mouth full of ugly, glistening teeth slither between the rails. I had no doubt it would climb the three little steps at the platform's end and devour me. I grabbed my mother's hand, too frightened to speak. Tears in my eyes. I looked up at her, pleading, and she gave me one of those 'it's all right, honey' smiles parents use when they see you're upset but don't know why. I pointed to the monster in the tunnel, and when I looked back at it, do you know what I saw?"

"I'm guessing not an alligator."

"A black trash bag blowing on the track. Our train pulled in then, funneling the air ahead of it, banishing that plastic bag into the subway depths. My mother hustled me onto the train. I never did tell her about my 'alligator' — but I never forgot it."

"Okay, but you saw what you saw because of the power of suggestion, the ideas your grandmother planted in your head. Your mind drew them onto a scrap of trash. How'd that lead you to cryptozoology?"

"The psychology of it isn't the part of the experience that stuck with me. It's the question, see? However briefly, I believed an alligator was on the train tracks. It was one hundred percent real to me until it wasn't, but it left a question in my mind. Could an alligator really survive a flush down the drain then live in the New York City sewers?"

"No, right? It would be caught in filters along the way or snagged at a treatment plant, and that's that."

"Did you know how sewers worked when you were in the second grade?"

"No."

"Me neither. Anyway, that's what got me hooked. And here is our exit."

Annetta's story had distracted us from the traffic, and now she guided her Prius up the exit ramp, off the Expressway. A fair number of cars and trucks came along and stayed with us. My parents often spoke about their trips out to Montauk or Orient Point, the South and North Forks of the Island when they were young, back when potato farms occupied more acreage than vineyards. Then city people and tourists "discovered" those places, the Hampton Jitney started shuttling eager, summer-struck Manhattanites on a regular schedule every Friday afternoon and Sunday morning, and everything changed. I imagined the place undeveloped, like Annetta's subway tunnel, a place where you could mistake a trash bag for a monster. An untamed place that had still existed not so long ago and maybe remained under the surface.

I don't know if it came down to Annetta's story setting the right mood, me simply getting caught up in her telling of it, or the shadows of the Pine Barrens, but barreling down Route 24, through Flanders, I believed that at the end of our drive, we might actually find that very special thing.

CHAPTER THREE

Later, cruising along Route 27, Sunrise Highway, we passed towns whose names I'd grown up with but had never visited. Shinnecock Hills. South Hampton. Sag Harbor. Amagansett. Rich-people places. Beach houses with backyard helipads. Montauk Shores' million-dollar trailer park homes. A place defined by stratospheric wealth where it seemed impossible a monster — or any other unattractive oddity — could long exist without some indignant plutocrat exterminating it for sullying their view of the Atlantic Ocean.

Some miles short of Ditch Plains Beach, where I'd assumed Annetta would want to stop, she turned north up Flamingo Avenue, where a peninsula poked into the Long Island Sound and formed the west side of Lake Montauk. Houses and residential streets surrendered to a stretch of wild overgrowth on either side of the road, a brief wild zone less than a mile long that drivers probably zipped through without noticing. The equivalent of rare vacant lots in the suburban sprawl. Still, the sudden emptiness echoed. The buzz of downtown Montauk, of traffic, of the "presence" of other people even when I couldn't see them, evaporated, leaving an almost tangible reverberation in my head. The psychic analog of how your ears ring after a rock concert. A sense of transition enhanced by a raft of gray clouds east of the road, the only blemish on an otherwise empty sky. They filtered the sunlight into hazy shafts that drilled into the trees.

Annetta made a sharp turn, slinging me in my seat. I hadn't even seen the driveway she entered, hadn't seen *any* connecting roads or turnoffs, as if this stubborn, wild patch refused entry to its secrets. Memories stirred of all those old fairy tales that warned of leaving the path — and yet an electric thrill ran through me at doing exactly that.

Intended for civilization, the Prius jounced harshly along the rugged trail. Annetta slowed to a crawl to save our teeth from rattling. Overgrown trees and shrubs closed on us. Branches clawed the car, scraped the windows.

"You sure this goes anywhere?" I said.

"Nope," Annetta said. "But these are the directions I received."

A muddy dip produced a bone-jarring, axle-busting bounce, but the Prius persevered and kept rolling. When the brush seemed ready to close up in a solid, dead-end wall, we lurched into a wide clearing. All the branches fell away, the ground smoothed, and Annetta guided the car to a stop outside a modest Cape Cod with a barn behind it and a muddy, beat-up Ford F150 pickup parked by the front door. We sat for a moment, relieved by the stillness.

"This the place?" I said.

"After all that? I sure hope so," Annetta said. "I need a break before trying to drive back down that road."

"Road? What road? There was a road? I totally missed that."

Annetta laughed, then cracked open her door and exited the car. I followed suit, emerging into hot, sticky air that smelled of damp earth and a strange gloom I hadn't noticed from inside the Prius. Those gray clouds had drifted over us. The sun floated behind them. Deep, late-morning shadows made the clearing look larger than I'd first thought, and the green beyond it seemed endless. My mind served up the odd caution that leaving here in any direction other than the one by which we'd come would lead to an infinite wilderness — a geographical impossibility, of course. No matter how isolated the place seemed, walking in any direction would soon lead to the shore, and in most directions, houses or roads before that. One of the quirks of living on an Island. That gave me no reassurance, though.

At the center of the clearing, the simple house, with brick steps to the front door, looked outdated enough to have started life as a fisherman's home a century ago. Weathered but well-maintained, it needed a fresh coat of paint and new roof shingles here and there, but it possessed a quaintness that suggested an inviting interior. Flower beds to either side of the stoop bloomed with marigolds and wild roses. I jotted the number beside the door, "712," in my notebook.

"Got the house number," I said.

Annetta smiled at me. "Good for you."

Behind the house, the barn trailed so far back into shadows, we couldn't see the other end of it. An optical illusion. Less well-kept than the house, the roof bowed, and the walls sagged a bit to the left, but the double-door entrance looked square to the earth, giving the structure a disjointed appearance.

The door of the house clacked open. A woman called out, "Good morning."

Annetta and I returned the greeting to a spry, elderly Asian woman with deep-set eyes and long gray hair tied back in a tight ponytail. She wore cargo shorts, a yellow-and-red floral print tank top, and sandals. Her broad smile displayed white teeth. Like the barn, she too looked out of sync, as if much older or younger than her appearance suggested. I couldn't decide which one.

She descended the front stoop. "Dr. Maikels?"

"That's me," Annetta said. "So nice to finally meet you, Ms. Sung."

"Likewise. Please call me Patricia. You made it just in time. Any trouble finding the place? Sometimes it's hard to see our driveway."

"No trouble at all," Annetta said. "Though I've been on roller coasters that bounced me around less."

Patricia frowned as if she didn't understand the reference. "Oh, uh-huh, I see, and who is this?"

I introduced myself. Patricia hugged each one of us as if greeting old friends. Annetta and I exchanged surprised glances but returned the hugs, afraid to offend her. Like a mother winding up a child to see Santa Claus, Patricia put her hands together and grinned.

"Are you ready to see a monster? You're not too scared, are you? Not a couple of fraidy-cats?"

We laughed, and Annetta declared us both ready and willing.

"Great!" Patricia clapped her hands. "First, though, come inside for some lunch."

"We're not really hungry. We'd love to have a look now," she said.

"Nonsense. You made a long trip. Come inside, eat, drink, and I'll tell you how I came to possess such an unusual thing. You won't be able to see it—really see it for what it is—if you don't hear my story first."

Weighing the burden of the long drive, the traffic, and the diminishing summer weekend, I bit back my impatience and followed Annetta's lead when she agreed. Patricia led us into her house. In the back of my mind, the dusty bones of childhood tales about strange houses in the woods rattled to life.

CHAPTER FOUR

Inside, Patricia's home matched the outside. Timeworn but neat and well-kept. Her husband, a burly man with a thick, red beard, sat in the living room watching a black-and-white movie on an old-fashioned tube TV. I wondered about the last time Marx Brothers movies had played on television and guessed some local station had put on a weekend marathon to spare the cost of contemporary programming. I pulled out my cell phone and searched for a Wi-Fi signal. None, though my mobile data showed four out of five bars, not bad for so far off the beaten path.

"That's Jack," Patricia said. "Say hello, Jack."

Jack looked away from the TV, smiled, and raised the can of Coors he held in one hand to greet us. He wore a white Rolling Stones T-shirt, their famous lips logo printed in red, and said, "Hey, there. Nice to meetcha."

His knobby, calloused hands, muscular arms, and weathered face suggested a retired fisherman. Not at all who I might have pictured married to Patricia. While she and Annetta walked on to the kitchen, Jack resumed watching TV, and I lingered, curious. It took me several seconds to figure out what sparked my interest: Jack's beer can opened with a pull tab that came completely free of the can; a teardrop sliver of aluminum lay curled on the side table by the sofa, the pull ring raised like an insect head. No company made cans like that anymore, not for decades, and I doubted unopened beer lasted that long. Maybe a kind of nostalgic, promotional can? Like classic Coke bottles at the holidays? Or—and I can't explain why I thought this then—the can was only a prop to make Jack look like an ordinary guy killing a Saturday afternoon. Absorbed by Groucho, Chico, and Harpo, he paid me no more attention, so I caught up to Annetta and Patricia in the linoleum-floored kitchen.

On an aluminum and Formica table sat plates of cold cuts and a loaf of Wonder Bread alongside bowls of potato salad and a dish of sliced cucumbers. A classic summer lunch served on retro furniture. Patricia gestured for us to sit then filled our glasses with iced tea from a Tupperware pitcher. Our paper plates, wedged into wicker holders to strengthen them, gave me a severe flashback to my youth when my mother had used those things at every family gathering until too much of the wicker broke, forcing her to give them up and buy sturdier paper plates.

"Go ahead and eat." Patricia speared the top half of the sliced roast beef with her fork and dropped it wholesale onto a piece of fluffy, white bread. "Don't worry about Jack. He ate a late breakfast."

She added an unappetizing full tablespoon of mayo to her sandwich and then squashed down the dollop with another slice of bread. I peeled off a few slices of turkey and some swiss, watched Annetta make a similar sandwich for herself, and then we each spooned some potato salad onto our plates. I grabbed a cucumber slice and then took a bite. Patricia lit up as we ate.

"Thank you for this lovely lunch, Patricia, but you promised us a story," Annetta said.

Patricia laughed. No, she guffawed. As if Annetta had quipped some knee-slapper, she rocked in her chair, her body shaking and her eyes turning watery. "Oh, yes, a story, the story." Her laughter died down. "I promised a story, and I keep my promises." None of us had more than sipped our iced tea, but Patricia topped us off, raising the liquid to the brim of our glasses. "It happened long ago, so you might think my memory isn't so great, or I might forget some details, but that isn't true. My memory is excellent. Jack can tell you I never forget a thing."

From the living room, Jack's hearty voice boomed out: "Memory like an elephant."

"Elephants never forget," Patricia said.

I could almost read Annetta's thoughts in her eyes. They mirrored my own. We'd driven hours to this out-of-the-way house to meet a woman who probably had nothing of substance to share. Nice, old Patricia Sung not only didn't have the Montauk Monster's remains but lacked a full deck as well. Still, I set my phone on the table and opened an audio recorder app to capture Patricia's story.

"No, I never forget. July 12, 2008, those girls took the picture. We've all seen it. Right? Everyone in the world gawked at it. They called it a monster. Now, a month ago, another picture. Same beach, same kind of critter. You've seen that one too? Of course, you have. Here's the thing you don't know. I discovered my Montauk Monster a long time ago, long before any of the others. Mine came first, and when I met it— it was alive. But *I* did not take a picture for the whole world to see."

Silence followed Patricia's revelation. I didn't know nearly as much about cryptozoology as Annetta, but I knew the most sensational claims almost always rose from hoaxes. Still, I scribbled notes and avoided Annetta's face, afraid to see disappointment in her expression.

"Okay, and, uh, where did you find it, Patricia?" Annetta asked.

"East of Ditch Plains Beach. They wash up all around here. A lot of them over the years, never found because the tide washed them back out, or raccoons ate them, or the sand covered them. Sometimes others came and dragged them back into the water and took them home. I knew where to look after the first one. More importantly, *how* to look. I have inside information. If you follow the tide charts and the ocean currents, if you watch the position of the stars and planets, check the weather, if you time things right, you can see them when they come. You can watch them in the water or on the shore. You must be quick, though. They never stay for long, and they don't like to be seen."

By this point, I'd set aside my food and glanced at Annetta. Almost as fascinating as Patricia's wild tale was the series of expressions on Annetta's face as she tried to reconcile it with her expectations.

"They've been coming here a long time. They like this place… love it, maybe, but they're afraid of people. So, they hide, keep away from lights and activity. It's dangerous for them in the water too. Fishermen. Sharks. Pollution. All those things keep them away. They still come back, though. They have to."

"Why is that?" Annetta said.

"Good question, ha-ha, yes, excellent question." Patricia leaned forward, chuckling. "After I found my first one, Jack helped me find others. We brought some home. The live ones never stayed with us long. The dead ones, well, that's why you came to visit."

"Are you saying you kept living Montauk Monsters like pets?" I said.

"Not pets, no. Guests. Friends. They came and went as they pleased."

"Your story is amazing, Patricia. Thank you for sharing it, but you remember what we discussed on the phone, right?" Annetta said.

"Proof," Patricia said. "Nothing counts without proof. I know. I used to be the same way."

"So, could we have a look at that proof now?"

Patricia shot her chair back from the table and snapped to her feet. Her odd sandwich remained untouched on her plate. "Of course. You didn't come all this way for nothing. Follow me." She dashed out the back door before we could rise and let the door slam shut behind her.

CHAPTER FIVE

Annetta and I exchanged glances as we hurried after Patricia to the barn. Those looks spoke volumes of disbelief, wonder, amusement, frustration, and resignation. We had come to see the remains and meant to do so before we left, to stick out the whole weird and staged experience. Even nature seemed in on it. Not a bird or a bug in sight on such a bright, hot day; those gray clouds hanging in the sky, unbothered by the wind. Patricia flickered in the odd, pale light the cloud shadows produced. The barn seemed even more off than before, as if it tilted now to the right, and then we stepped inside, into a scene neither of us expected.

Squirrels, rabbits, seagulls, raccoons, possums, osprey, and two dozen more types of animals, all well preserved, sat carefully displayed in dioramas of their natural settings. On the walls hung display cases of insects, moths, butterflies, and spiders. Shelves filled with boxes of varying sizes and shapes stood at the back of the barn, behind a large table overloaded with knives, sewing materials, stand-up magnifying glasses, and other taxidermy tools. Sawdust spread thick on the earthen floor softened our footsteps, and exuded a mellow, woodsy odor into the air. Everything seemed quieter inside the barn, sounds sinking into its wood planks and the deep gloom overhead. For the first time, the possibility of seeing a true Montauk Monster, a creature unknown to science, loomed real to me.

"This collection is amazing," Annetta said. "You did all this?"

"With help from Jack. Collecting specimens is our hobby, although Jack leaves all the messy work to me, all the stuffing and sewing. He doesn't like that part, but I feel closer to the animals that way."

While Patricia gave Annetta a run-through of her equipment, I toured the displays, admiring the lifelike quality of each preserved mammal or bird, and snapped photos for my article, many more than I knew they would use, but I wanted them for myself. I saw no reptiles or amphibians. All the bugs were pinned inside their cases, looking less lively than the stuffed mammals—except when I peered into the spider collection. One twitched its leg. A trick of the light had created a sense of motion, I thought—but the leg moved again. My stomach knotted. I never liked spiders. Though I knew most spiders posed zero threat to people, that primal fear of the alien, the strange, the inhuman, lived well and hearty in my psyche. The idea of living specimens made my skin crawl. I retreated from the case but hesitated as I noticed gaps in the display's wooden frame. Enough for the soft breeze passing through the barn wall slats to breathe life into a dead arachnid? Quite possibly.

My relief proved fleeting, though, when I noticed two of Patricia's specimens possessed extra pairs of legs—twelve each, rather than eight—and that those bonus legs ended in tiny, three-pronged pincers. That pushed me over the line. I hurried away, turning my attention to a chipmunk forever clambering up a branch and a pair of ducks floating on a clear acrylic pond. Another display case held no animals, only a dozen tufts of coarse, brown hair that shimmered in the light, each sample labeled for a different state.

Patricia appeared beside me. "All my specimens are local except for those."

I hadn't heard her approach because of how the barn dampened sound, and her voice startled me. The idea of those twelve-legged spiders as part of the local fauna made my throat tighten. All I could manage to say was, "You've done amazing work preserving them."

Patricia nodded. "I show them respect."

From the storage shelves, she gathered three shoeboxes, large enough to hold men's work boots, and brought them to her worktable. Annetta and I joined her. With a wide grin, Patricia carefully removed the lid of each box and set them aside. "Here is the main attraction."

I snapped pictures of Annetta peering into the containers, of Patricia beaming like a proud artist, of the boxes open with their lids beside them like tiny, disinterred coffins, and then I looked for myself. Each box held a collection of clean bones. I identified those I could: ribs, toes, spine, and skull. Some I didn't recognize, nor could I catalog the scattered bits and pieces that I guessed made sense only with muscle and ligament to hold them in place. The bones told me nothing, an anticlimactic experience. All that time driving, all that build-up, and I didn't possess the knowledge to know whether I looked at raccoon or cat skeletons or something extraordinary. Only the skulls suggested anything unusual to me.

Little shovel heads with jaws lined at the back by rows of human-like teeth that gave way to a bony beak with razor-sharp edges. What animal possessed both teeth and a beak? A platypus, perhaps. Some kind of bird? I didn't know, and these teeth looked too human for comfort except for pairs of nasty canines at the back of the jaw. I overcame my revulsion and shot pictures from every angle, zoomed in to seek out telltale signs of fabrication with my lens. Thread, dried glue, pins, anything holding together a hoax. But nothing revealed itself.

"What do you think?" I asked Annetta.

Her wide-eyed face spoke volumes. "Patricia, you can tell when they'll appear again?"

"If you pay attention, you can see the signs."

"Can you teach me how to read these signs?"

Patricia frowned, shook her head. "Takes years to learn."

"How about telling us the next time they'll come around?" I asked.

"Maybe." Patricia shrugged. "If they want me to."

"If who wants you too, the Montauk Monsters?" Annetta asked.

"They sometimes let me bring people to see them. Not often. It took years before they let Jack come along. They trust me. Trust him now too. I can ask them about you."

My camera clicked and whirred as I snapped more images of the barn, of Annetta and Patricia, of the animal displays, of the storage shelves, recording as much as possible. When I'd exhausted photographic possibilities, I switched to video mode and shot a tour of Patricia's work. I even forced myself back to the spider case. Sunlight dappled through holes in the roof, creating flashes of brightness that skimmed across the camera's screen, lending everything a sense of unreality.

"That's enough for today. Time for you to go now," Patricia said.

"Not yet," Annetta said. "I have so many questions for you. I need a bone sample for DNA testing. Could I take a small piece with me?"

"Oh, no, those bones are part of my collection. I won't part with even a scrap of them," Patricia said. "I'm tired now. Need to rest. Thank you for coming. I hope this helps you."

I continued shooting video as Patricia ushered us from the barn toward Annetta's car, recorded the house, the pickup truck, the thick brush, and the gray clouds hanging between us and the sun.

"I need more information," Annetta said. "A closer look at the remains, microscopic and spectroscopic analysis, opinions from other scientists. It must be documented, Patricia. The provenance recorded. The exact location of where you found them. How old they are. Please, without proof, none of this counts. I can pay you for your time if that's what you need."

"I don't need money," Patricia said. "I need rest. You have your proof."

"No, Patricia, I need to take proof with me to show others."

"You have *your* proof." Patricia smiled and squeezed Annetta's shoulder. "Maybe I'll call you later. You can come back another day."

"But we're here now," Annetta said.

The front door banged open. Jack appeared on the stoop, his stocky musculature tense. No trace of a friendly grin remained on his face. One hand gripped a Coors can, crumpled in the middle, Jack's fingers squeezing it, opening, squeezing, opening, squeezing, each grip crinkling the aluminum.

Annetta frowned at Jack. I stopped my video and clicked several pictures of him.

"All right, I'll call you tomorrow," Annetta said. "Thank you for today, for your hospitality, for the tour, for sharing your story."

"You're welcome. Live for the day, right? Go now before it gets too late. We'll talk soon, maybe."

We slid into the Prius. Annetta started the car then waved as she guided it to the dirt trail. I kept taking pictures as we moved away, then switched back to video and recorded our ride out to the main road. Neither of us spoke a word, too wrapped up in trying to make sense of our visit. After stopping where dirt met pavement, Annetta punched the gas. The Prius sped south along Flamingo Avenue, the sky now crystal clear, the sun brilliant, unobscured, the raft of gray clouds vanished as if they'd never existed.

Questions swirled in my head, a dozen different things to ask Annetta, but I kept quiet. Her brow furrowed, and her lips formed silent words, warning me not to interrupt her thoughts. I only hoped, if she did return here on another day, she'd bring me with her.

CHAPTER SIX

An hour later, in a booth in a diner off Sunrise Highway, I looked up from my phone.

"Platypus don't have teeth."

From the seat across the table, Annetta's face scrunched. "What?"

"That thing had teeth *and* a beak. Like, human or dog teeth. What kind of animal has that? Some birds have teeth, right? But not teeth like that thing had. They're ridges along the beak. That thing looked like it needed annual dental check-ups."

"You're fixated on its teeth?"

"I'm out of my depth here, Annetta. You've hardly said boo. I need some handle on all this because if you looked up 'weird' in the dictionary, our afternoon might be there as an example. Who the hell eats mayonnaise that way?"

Annetta laughed and stirred her coffee. The diner windows overlooked the parking lot and the road. Cars came and went. People walked by, and the steady noise of the diner rattled on, broken now and then by a child's laugh or a waitress calling out an order behind the counter. At that moment, I lived in a different world than Annetta. Her mind wandered places I'd never gone, never knew existed. When she looked at me, she did so with a clinical eye studying a specimen, a piece of a puzzle for her to fit into place, into a bigger picture only she perceived. Our order came. I put down my phone and ate, taking comfort in a cheeseburger deluxe and the familiarity of French fries. Annetta's plate went untouched. She only swirled her spoon round and round in her coffee, metal clinking ceramic with the tone of a distant wind chime.

"Hey, serious question, are you all right?" No answer. "We saw some strange stuff out there, I know, but I'm thinking Jack in his tutu and faerie wings took the prize. Or maybe Patricia doing that bikini dance with a snake on her shoulders. Did they really strike you as the kind of people who'd own a Ferrari?"

The spoon stopped. Annetta's gaze, which had focused on some faraway point outside the window and past the horizon, turned to me. Her lips creased in a slow smile, and then she burst out laughing.

"I'm sorry, Ben. You caught me lost in my thoughts. I didn't mean to be so rude."

"No worries, Doc. We did see some pretty odd stuff."

"The whole experience was odd."

"No argument there."

"Even how Ms. Sung contacted me was odd. I had my suspicions when she first reached out. How did she find me? Why did she choose *me* to show her monster remains? I'm not famous. I'm not local. The only people who know of my interest in cryptozoology are my friends and family, none of whom, as far as I know, have ever trekked out to this crazy chunk of the Island. Online friends know about it too. I'm in several groups, acquaintances with a few well-known cryptozoologists. That's how I met Ethan. So, how did she find me?"

"Maybe she's in the same groups. She said she's been doing this a long time, the taxidermy, following the Montauk Monsters and all."

"Yeah, or maybe someone in those groups who doesn't know New York geography referred her to me thinking Brooklyn and Montauk were close, being on the same island. There's another possibility, and that's what's got me so preoccupied. Have you heard of *high strangeness*?"

"Is that a band or a drug reference?"

Annetta shook her head. "J. Allen Hynek coined the term. He was one of the original UFO investigators. Worked for the Air Force investigating flying saucers. He was a consultant on *Close Encounters of the Third Kind*. He created the whole scale of close encounters with alien phenomena."

"Never heard of him. My mom likes that movie, though. What's this got to do with Ms. Sung?"

"Did anything about our visit there seem normal to you?"

I found myself at a loss. I didn't dwell much on ideas of "normal" or "abnormal." They seemed outdated, the kind of notions that made sense before the Internet pumped into our faces every weird obsession and fetish, every off-beat lifestyle, and all the unique ways people chose to live or seek attention. With the right keywords, I could find half a dozen stranger living scenarios on the first page of my search results.

"High strangeness is a pervasive sense of absurdity, illogic, or oddity. It's most often associated with UFO investigations, but other investigators have reported it too. John Keel wrote about it in his book on the Mothman. It's lost time, disjointed reality, and obsessions with seemingly meaningless, often mundane details. Tell me Ms. Sung wasn't going overboard to convince us she and Jack live an everyday, normal life. I mean, who the hell eats Wonder Bread anymore? And the Marx Brothers on TV? It's like someone from 1982 came out of hibernation."

To Annetta's list, I added the wind-immune, gray clouds hanging nearby, how the barn leaned one way then the other, the pull-top Coors can, and the way Jack worked it in his hand. A different picture formed. "I see what you're saying, but why does it matter? People are weird."

With a sigh, Annetta looked out the window. No answer. We didn't talk much more as we ate. When we finished, Annetta drove us to Ditch Plains Beach to the site where those girls had first photographed the original Montauk Monster. Sand and water. Beachgoers. Surfers. Seagulls. On the horizon, fishing boats. I shot a ton of pictures perfect for travel brochures, but little help in proving the existence of monsters. After an hour, we left, passing signs for Camp Hero State Park to the east near the famous Montauk Lighthouse at the very end of Long Island's South Fork. Nothing beyond that but the Atlantic Ocean.

Annetta pulled to the side of the road. "Let's go back. Let's go see Ms. Sung again before we head home. Put their address in your GPS."

"Are you sure that's a good idea? Jack seemed pretty tense when we left."

"Don't worry about it. Just go. I want to see something."

I plugged 712 Flamingo Avenue into my navigation app. No such address came up. I tried different numbers in different orders, thinking I'd misremembered, but still nothing. I zoomed in—satellite view, street view—looking for the house, that pitted dirt road. In that whole patch of wild through which we'd driven, not a single residence appeared. Only a single two-lane road, scrub brush, and trees, houses to the north and south, water east and west.

"It's like they're not on the map," I said.

"Right, exactly."

"You knew that? How did you find them this morning?"

Pulling a folded piece of paper from inside the center console, Annetta showed me handwritten directions. "Patricia gave me directions over the phone. When you asked me for the address, I didn't have it. She never told me. I'll bet that house number was phony. They hung it up to mislead us."

"I'm not sure if that makes them or you paranoid. Okay, so we follow your directions."

"We can try, but Patricia was very clear about the timing of our visit."

I didn't understand then why that mattered beyond common courtesy. Annetta put the car in drive. We zipped onto the road, back to Flamingo Avenue. We drove that wild stretch, one end to the other and back again, then retraced our path. Nowhere did we find that dirt driveway that led to the house. At about the place we agreed it had been, Annetta parked on the shoulder, and we walked into the brush. Nothing. No sign of a house or a barn, of a dirt road or a pickup truck. Above us, a sharp, empty sky. Around us, shadows deepening as the afternoon wore on.

We stood in the thick of the overgrowth, bees buzzing the wildflowers and birds calling from the trees. The world seemed as normal as possible, so unlike what we'd experienced earlier that I finally gleaned some idea of what "high strangeness" meant. Patricia Sung had said, *You made it just in time. Sometimes it's hard to see our driveway.* A chill ran through me, raising goose bumps on my arms. Annetta's face enlivened as if she'd made some pivotal discovery that she didn't much like—but weeks would pass before I understood what concerned and excited her so much.

CHAPTER SEVEN

A week later, my article posted online. The editor ran half a dozen of my best photos but cut the text to the bone and turned it into a series of extended captions, all mention of oddness, gray clouds, and can-crushing fishermen excised, and Ms. Sung described as "an eccentric naturalist." He shifted the slant to her taxidermy work and included a few select quotes from Annetta that made her sound skeptical of the Montauk Monster. The new angle painted us as myth debunkers. Nothing untrue, but a representation quite different than the reality. Behold the power of the press. Factual, perhaps, but false. At least my check cleared, so I brought Ethan lunch to celebrate and thank him for the connection.

By mid-July, he managed to hobble around on crutches, and his chest didn't ache every time he took a deep breath. His girlfriend, Lana, joined us for diner take-out — good, greasy, comfort food. Ethan had read the article and complimented me on my photos. He knew the editor, Joshua Malachy, better than I did, so it didn't surprise me when he asked me what really happened that day. I gave him the story as I'd written it. He and Lana hung on every word until I ran out of them, and we'd reduced our burgers and fries to scraps.

Ethan scowled, disappointed. "I had a feeling it was going to be the real deal."

"More like the unreal deal." I wiped my lips with a napkin then dropped it on the remains of my meal. "Wait, you mean you believe all that stuff?"

"Don't you?" Ethan looked shocked. "You saw it all firsthand."

I shrugged. "Was it weird? Hell, yeah. Did it seem like the place vanished off the face of the Earth? Uh-huh. Did it really? Come on, how could that happen? We missed it, or took a wrong turn, or, who knows, maybe Ms. Sung and her husband dragged brush onto the road to camouflage it like in some old movie after we left."

"You think that's probable?" Ethan said.

"More probable than the place disappearing into thin air. Annetta drove us out there after memorizing Patricia Sung's directions. We can't be sure we exactly duplicated the route coming from another starting point. We might have wound up on a similar-looking road. Her idea about a phony house number makes more sense to me than whatever the heck you're thinking, which is what exactly?"

Ethan slurped soda through a straw.

"That sounds like rationalizing," Lana said.

"You believe this stuff too?"

"What 'stuff' is that?" Ethan asked.

"I don't know, UFOs, astral projection, mental telepathy, ESP, clairvoyance, spirit photography, telekinetic movement, full trance mediums, the Loch Ness Monster, and the theory of Atlantis," I said, grinning.

Ethan and Lana laughed. "If there's a steady paycheck in it, I'll believe anything you say," she said.

"Yeah, yeah, it's easy to make fun and quote *Ghostbusters*, but, seriously, Ben, what do you think we believe that you find so frightening?" asked Ethan.

"I'm not frightened."

"People make fun of stuff that scares them," Ethan said.

"True. They also make fun of stuff that's, you know, risible."

Ethan's smile flattened as he slumped back in his seat. I regretted the comment but not the sentiment. Since my visit to Ms. Sung's, I'd thought everything through many times, found mundane explanations for almost every strange thing I'd experienced. An elderly couple set in their ways, unaccustomed to visitors. The early stages of some form of dementia. Annetta playing a joke on me, hustling to give me a better story in hopes of gaining publicity for herself. I couldn't discount Annetta's infectious enthusiasm or the fact that she intimidated and attracted me so much that I found everything she said fascinating. That didn't make the impossible possible, though, and I'd put that part of it behind me. Annetta and I kept in touch, but we didn't talk much about Monty or Ms. Sung. Mostly, I made up "research" questions that gave me an excuse to email her or chat on the phone every few days. I don't think she minded. It never occurred to me before then that Ethan took these things to heart.

"Hey, man, I'm sorry. I didn't mean that as a putdown. You gave me a great opportunity with that story, and I'm grateful."

"I know," Ethan said. "I don't mean to be so touchy. My pain meds put me on edge. I'm not asking because I want to convince you. I needed to know you take it seriously enough to write an honest story. You did great with the Montauk Monster. Malachy slipped me your unedited piece. You gave the whole thing fair coverage. I just wanted to hear it from you."

"That's the job, right? Report the story. Let the readers decide, or the editor wield the red pen. Why are you so concerned, though?"

Ethan straightened his back and adjusted his broken leg, still encased in a cast. "I have another lead for you. A tip that came to me. I can't follow up on it, but I don't want to let it go cold. Something about it feels different than the usual whacko tips about this stuff. Guy's a retired sheriff, sterling record, straight shooter. I don't think he's making anything up. Whatever he's experiencing is real. He just can't figure out what it is."

"Where do you get these tips, Ethan? Editors drop this stuff in the round file."

"It didn't come through the paper," Ethan said.

"I run an online group about paranormal occurrences and weird phenomena," Lana said. "People post things there. Every so often, one reaches out with questions. A skeptic who's exhausted all other options for an explanation."

"You really are the Ghostbusters," I said.

"No, no ghosts," Lana said. "I don't believe in them. I like crypto-zoology and ufology. Weird stuff with a potentially scientific explanation. Undiscovered species. Aliens. I do weird weather and mysterious places too. Frog rains, Bermuda Triangle, that kind of stuff. Right? No haunted houses or cursed dolls."

"You're into this too?" I asked Ethan.

"It's how we met. We hit it off in the group, started chatting. Our first long weekend together, we drove up to Lake Champlain to look for Champy."

"Who's that?"

"The Lake Champlain Monster. New York's version of Nessie," Lana said.

"You find him?"

Lana grinned. "We didn't spend all that much time looking to tell you the truth. Found better ways to spend the time, mostly in our room."

"Oof, okay, TMI, gotcha. So, this sheriff, he lives on Long Island? I take this story, am I going to get paid for it? Not that I'm reluctant to help you guys with your Scooby-Doo mystery-solving, but I need to make rent and eat too."

"I set it up at the paper. Count on Malachy cutting it down to a photo slideshow again, but, yeah, he's up for it. Your piece on Monty got serious clicks. Your photos catch the eye, keep people clicking through the slideshow. This is good for you. Deliver another strong piece, and they might hire you as a staff photographer," Ethan said.

"Guess I owe you another thank you followed by a second glorious feast of cheeseburgers and diner fries when the check clears," I said. "Tell me about the tip."

Chapter Eight

Most everyone on Long Island knows about the Big Duck. A roadside duck farm stand built in the shape of an enormous duck in 1931, it long ago earned landmark status and lent its name to the architecture lexicology, where a "big duck" means any structure designed to resemble its purpose. Not exactly the kind of thing you'd expect to mark your last stop for civilization, but a few days after lunch with Ethan and Lana, I sped past the Duck on my way into one of the largest patches of the Pine Barrens. Sheriff Malik Campbell lived off Red Creek Road, just east of Hubbard County Park. A house on the edge of one of Long Island's few large stretches of true wilderness. Admiring the Duck's novelty as I drove through those empty woods, I wished Annetta had come with me, but a summer symposium had taken her out of town for a week, and Ethan insisted I jump on his lead right away.

At what felt to me like the heart of this stretch of the Barrens, I parked on the shoulder and stepped out of the car to stretch my legs and shoot some photos. The tree shadows caught my eyes, and I couldn't pass up the lighting. Hazy, hot, and humid, as the weathermen like to say, on those oppressive summer days, and we'd had a lot of them this July. Sweat beads rushed to formation on my forehead. Insects buzzed in the brush and trees. Bees flitted around patches of clover and wild honeysuckle. I looked both ways down the road. No cars in sight. No planes humming or roaring overhead. No human voices in range. I knew the wilderness only spanned so far before it ran up against another road or the Long Island Sound, but I believed I could get lost in there, wander for days, never be found, as if walking among those hills and trees meant entering another world. I shot a couple dozen photos and then, wiping sweat from my brow, settled back into the air-conditioned coolness of my car. Fifteen minutes later, I pulled up a gravel driveway at Sheriff Campbell's house, a ranch with yellow vinyl siding, and an attached two-car garage. A lanky, black man in a pair of faded jeans and a T-shirt the color of a clear sky sat on the front porch, shaded, holding a silver travel mug in one hand.

"You Benjamin Keep?" he called as I exited my car.

"Yes, sir. Nice to meet you, Sheriff Campbell."

"Can that 'Sheriff' stuff, son. I'm retired. Call me Malik."

He set his mug on a table and met me in front of the house. Gray streaks ran through his tight-cut afro, and deep, serious lines on his face gave him a look of weathered experience. We shook hands, his grip crushing and assertive. He looked dry as a bone, unbothered by the stifling, hazy air.

"Thanks for coming. I'd really hoped Ethan could make it. How's he doing?"

"Healing well. Should be up on his feet again in a few weeks."

"Glad to hear it. I don't normally put much stock in those weird creatures and aliens he's into, but he makes some sense on that forum where I found him. Kind of level-headed. Just the facts. Like me. Got to have evidence that holds up to scrutiny. Tell you this, son, you go into court with weak evidence, a defense lawyer will shred you and sprinkle you on kibble for his dog, then, poof, your case gets chewed to pieces, the prosecutor resents you, a whole bad scene. I appreciate anyone who understands the importance of good evidence."

"I hear you. That's why I'm here."

"Excellent, because I've got a ton of evidence. I just don't know what the hell it adds up to. This thing has been stalking my property for a couple of months now, howling in the Barrens at night, knocking branches against tree trunks, leaving deer carcasses on my property, banging and scratching on my back door, scat everywhere. Drove off my wife. She's staying with her sister in Yaphank until I get this settled."

"What do you think it is?"

"I figured critters, but the only one that made sense is a bear, and there are no bears on Long Island. So, a group of kids, I thought. Bored teenagers screwing around, stoned or drunk. Except the sounds coming out of those woods, they ain't nothing human. And, yeah, I considered they were playing a recording or using a device to alter their voices, but, well, you hear those sounds, you'll understand. They drill through you like an icicle. Then there's the stink. Like an open sewer or a ripe garbage dump. Foul enough to make you retch."

"Sounds awful." I slung my camera across my shoulder then clipped a microphone to my shirt collar. A new gadget I'd picked up, it connected to my phone via Bluetooth, recording everything I or anyone within ten feet or so of me said onto my phone. "When did this start?"

"Middle of May. Kind of low-key, quiet, weird, but not frightening. Then right around the third week in June, off the charts. That's when they tried to get into the house. Come on, I'll show you."

Malik led the way to the back door. The screen in the storm door hung in ribbons. A powerful force had left the door's aluminum frame bent and deformed. Behind it, splintery scratches marred the interior door, and the whole thing looked caved in as if a heavy weight had thrust against it several times, shoving the door almost off its hinges. The vinyl siding bore similar marks. I focused my camera and shot photos.

"This assault lasted maybe ten minutes."

I lowered my camera. "You're telling me someone tried to break into your house?"

Malik shook his head. "I'm telling you some-*thing* tried to. Afterward, I heard howling in the Barrens, the knocking of wood against wood. Next morning, Janae packed a suitcase and lit out for her sister's. Since then, it's been constant, every night, but it hasn't assaulted my house again, at least."

"When did the assault occur?"

Malik told me the date and time. After dark on the same Saturday Annetta and I had visited Ms. Sung. Coincidence, nothing more. Except if you asked Ethan, Lana, or the people who followed them online, no such thing existed. Everything happened for a reason. Everything connected. Synchronicities, they called it. The confluence of seemingly unrelated events that hinted at deeper meanings invisible on the surface of things. And here stood retired Sheriff Malik Campbell, showing me proof that a monster had tried to break into his house. Unbelievable testimony from reliable witnesses. A hallmark of so many reports of cryptids, UFOs, and other weird phenomena, which I'd read about in-depth since my day trip with Annetta. Nothing about Malik raised doubt or pointed to a scam. The tone of his voice and his calm demeanor suggested he didn't care if I bought his story because he knew its truth.

"Let me ask you this," he said. "You believe? Like Ethan and Lana do? They take this stuff for fact. Do a nice job sifting the wheat from the chaff and pointing out some interesting stories that maybe defy easy explanation, but, end of the day, they're all-in on the reality of these weird creatures or whatevers. Me, I've seen strange things, especially on the job. None that couldn't be explained by human stupidity, malice, or heavy substance abuse."

"I guess you could call me skeptical but open-minded," I said.

"An open mind is good. That's me too. Okay, let me show you a few more things."

We walked the edge of Malik's property, drifting into the periphery of the Pine Barrens at times. I recorded it all on my camera. Trees with bark gouged away in vertical scratches that started about twelve feet up their trunk. Piles of dried scat that looked like the work of a Great Dane that beat its masters to a fully set Thanksgiving dinner. I knew nothing about identifying animals by their droppings, and the piles buzzed with flies, so I snapped quick pictures to show Annetta when she returned. Quite the romantic gesture, I know. But the most startling thing on our tour was the footprints. Five-toed, human-like, bigger than the biggest pair of clown shoes I could imagine, they sank inches deep into the soft summer soil. Left, right, left, right, into the Barrens, suggesting a stride longer than my full height when I stood up straight. The prints awed me. I measured them with a tape measure from Malik. Twenty-three inches long, nine inches wide. Then I photographed them from every angle. The part of my mind that paid the bills and set my alarm clock every night spoke of all the obvious explanations for such prints. Another part of my mind, a remnant of my youth when everything in my room changed after the lights switched off, a part stirred from hibernation by my adventure at Ms. Sung's, sent electric thrills along my spine. That part of me intuited the inherent reality of them, and then my stomach clenched, and my breathing turned shallow.

Everything in the woods changed then. I looked up from my camera screen. The trees seemed taller, the Barrens deeper, and the air quieter and laden with something more than cloying moisture. A faint, foul odor tickled at my nostrils. I gazed back at Malik's house, almost out of sight through the woods, and couldn't recall walking so far from it. My sense of time and distance deteriorated. My mind wrestled over whether I'd simply lost track or the ground had stretched out behind us, drawing us farther from safety, from civilization, from the world of known things.

Most of all, in that moment, I felt watched, studied, noticed, and acknowledged.

The steady film of perspiration on my forehead burst into an all-out sweat. Drops ran down my face. I trembled as a wave of lightheadedness dizzied me. I shuffled my feet to keep my balance. The incredible footprints continued on and on into the Barrens, but the idea of following them any farther made my heart race.

"You feel it?" Malik said. "Gets you right in the gut and deep down in your brain, right? The world seems different. More threatening. Uncertain. You feel smaller. You feel something watching us?"

"Yeah," I said. "Yeah, I do."

"Welcome to my world," Malik said, his voice suddenly bright and wryly cheerful, giving over to a short bout of laughter. "Welcome to Bigfoot on Long Island."

Chapter Nine

I agreed to stay the night at Malik's out of fear of missing out on the chance to document something beyond incredible — and the opportunity to share my discovery with Annetta. Since I'd met her, any excuse to talk or spend time with her seemed to outweigh most other considerations. A Bigfoot hunt would provide fuel for countless conversations.

Around twilight, Malik worked the gas grill behind his house while I sat at the patio table and watched shadows change in the woods. The sky remained clear, and as the darkness deepened, stars flickered to life. We drank Rolling Rocks and ate grilled chicken and fresh salad, simple food that still boasted of Malik's skills as a cook.

"There are two ways we can go about this," he said, pushing his empty plate aside, washing down his last bite with a swig of beer. "One, we spend the night in the house, keep watch at the windows, and hope it comes in close enough for you to take a picture or record it or whatever. Two, we sit up in my truck parked off to the side of the property near the footprints. That'll give us a better vantage on the Barrens as well as the house."

"A stakeout," I said.

Malik smiled. "That's right."

My instinct for self-preservation campaigned for staying in the house; my hope for spectacular proof of Malik's nocturnal harasser lobbied for the truck. Hope won over fear. After clearing up from dinner, we settled in as far from the house and as close to the woods as Malik could park his Toyota Tundra. I sat in the truck bed, camera ready, recorder on, with Malik holding vigil in the driver's seat, ready to rush toward the road if the thing tried to do to his truck what it had done to his back door. Hope dwindled as hours dragged on. In my boredom, I concocted scenario after scenario for Malik destroying his own back door as part of a Bigfoot hoax. I doubted he had, but it entertained me and becalmed the voice in my head calling me an idiot for wasting time on this and begging me to go home and sleep in my own bed. The summer night wheeled on, though. The humidity lessened. Distant fireworks cracked and boomed. The mosquitoes died down after full dark. None of the rustling coming from the woods sounded like anything more than possums and raccoons.

"They come around at any particular time?" I asked.

"Hold on, let me check my Bigfoot schedule," Malik said.

"Ha-ha," I said.

"Late, that's all. Never before midnight."

I checked my watch, 12:32 a.m. "Anytime now, I guess."

"They don't come every night. Haven't been around the last two nights, though, so I figure chances are good for tonight."

By three a.m., Malik's assessment seemed off. I wondered if I'd stepped into a scenario I'd read about repeatedly since diving in on the Montauk Monster. Compelling physical evidence. A sense of something unreal in the air. But never any sign of cryptid activity when you're looking for it. Like the creatures knew better than to show up for cameras and additional witnesses. Cryptozoology's elusive nature frustrated me. In many ways, it struck me like astrology, reading things into the stars and taking it on faith they meant something. Only the existence of a few true proven cryptids, the coelacanth, and the giant squid, for example, kept me from closing the door on possibilities. That and the fact that Annetta, certainly smarter than me with her Ph.D. and scientific expertise, never closed that door either.

By 3:30 a.m., though, my eyes hung heavy, and my body begged for sleep. I had enough for a story, for another click-bait slideshow to please Malachy and show Ethan I'd put in the effort. My head dipped as I nodded off for a moment. A rotten stink snapped me awake.

Malik thumped on the roof. "Smell that?"

"Like something died out there."

"It's coming."

The odor ripened, tying my stomach in queasy knots. Then the knocking came, the unmistakable sound of wood cracking against wood, a boy hitting a tree trunk with a baseball bat, but amplified, enlarged, a branch instead of a bat, swung with the awe-inspiring strength of inhuman muscles. The clacking echoed through the Barrens, three whacks then a pause, three whacks then a pause, the volume rising as the source approached Malik's home. The brush rustled and shook. I strained my eyes to see into the darkness.

"Hand me a flashlight," I said.

"Hell no," Malik said. "That'll drive it off for sure. Be patient."

I checked the night- and low-light settings on my camera, held my breath, and scanned the woods and the silhouette of Malik's house. The stench wrapped around us like an ashy film, coating everything. The knocking intensified, the pause between each series of whacks shortening. Then came a string of nine hits against a tree trunk. After that, everything turned silent. Insects stopped chirping. The soft breeze faded to stillness. The world felt suppressed. Withdrawn.

A shape emerged from the woods maybe forty yards from the truck.

Camouflaged in shadow, it stood at least nine feet tall. A column of muscle and hair that shouldered out of the trees as if it pressed against saplings instead of decades-old growth.

I snapped pictures, checked my recorder.

At the first minute click of my camera, the thing howled. It moved, faster than should've been possible for anything that size, and then a four-foot branch, inches thick and stripped of bark, came whirling out of the darkness and sailed at my head. I dropped to the truck bed. The branch missed me and thumped to the ground on the other side of the truck.

"It threw that!" I shouted.

"It does that. Keep your head down. Stop yelling," Malik said.

The massive shape stepped toward us. Another howl sent its voice needling through me and turned my blood cold, convincing me Malik spoke true that no human or recording could produce that sound. It shook the air. It reverberated in my skin, my bones, my mind. I absorbed it as much as heard it, a revolting sensation. It took another step, stomped the ground twice, and then rushed us.

Malik ignored his own admonition to keep quiet and cried out, "Oh, shit!"

The truck engine roared to life. Malik threw it in gear and slammed the gas. The abrupt motion threw me on my back. I laid down in the truck bed, grabbed my camera on its tripod, and hugged it beside me as I pressed my feet to the walls to pin myself in place. The truck swerved then skidded to a sharp stop. A branch fell from the sky, clipped the tailgate with a jarring crunch, then bounced away.

I lifted my head. The thing stood directly in front of the truck. Malik had braked maybe fifty feet from it. The headlights painted its shaggy legs, muscular beyond anything human and thick, with silvery, matted fur that shimmered and danced with ribbons and lashes of faint iridescence.

"How'd it get in front of us?" I asked.

"It didn't!" Malik said.

A howl from behind us ripped the night and drew my attention to where the first one stood, stamping its foot into the ground. The thump of it boomed in my ears, its strength trembling the earth so hard the vibrations reached me even in the truck. One behind us, one in front of us, both threatening, monstrous. From back in the Barrens came yet more howls and the fresh clack of branches against tree trunks.

"There's more?" I shouted

"We have to move. Get down and hold on!" Malik called.

The truck lurched left, the tires spun for a second, and then it surged into the night. Hunkered in the truck bed, hanging onto my camera, to the side of the truck, I saw only flashes of night, stars, and shadows, heard the roar of the engine, the howls of the creatures, the drumming crack of wood. Malik slalomed, tossing me from one side of the bed to the other, and then abruptly, the ride smoothed out and shot forward in a straight line. I lifted my camera above the side of the truck and snapped blind pictures in hopes of catching something, anything that might show what we'd encountered.

The truck bounced onto the road. Malik's property fell out of sight.

He didn't stop driving until we reached the only all-night gas station in the area, with its lights and neon Budweiser and Lotto signs offering a welcome defense against the dark. There he parked, and there we stayed until morning when the time came to return to Malik's and see what we'd left behind.

Chapter Ten

Giant footprints littered Malik's backyard, almost as disconcerting in the morning light as the creatures themselves. Malik and I identified several sets of prints, all within a couple of inches' range for length and width. Where the things had stomped, the prints sank six inches into the soil. We collected the sticks thrown at us and dumped them in the truck bed. Then Malik surveyed his house and found no damage done. I photographed everything then recorded video while I walked the lines of prints back to the Barrens, stopping at the edge, terrified to set foot within that wilderness even on a sunny morning.

Malik came out of his house with mugs of steaming coffee and handed me one. "Still got an open mind?"

I laughed. "I feel like I lived Ethan's dream."

"I say it's a nightmare." Malik slurped coffee then let out a long breath. "So, where do we go from here? What are our next steps? Set up trail cameras? Microphones? Try to trap one of them?"

Frowning, I said, "What are you talking about?"

"You got the story of a lifetime here, Ben. You see that, right? Footprints and blurry photographs won't convince anyone except those who already believe. You got to seize the bull by the horns, son. Prove it. Document this for the world. And most important? Get these damn things off my property."

I hadn't considered anything more than heading home and filing my story for Malachy to slice and dice and twist into clickbait, fuel for some late-night TV comedy host's crazy headlines bit. *So, I hear Bigfoot's now summering in the Hamptons. He heard Spielberg has a place out there and has a script he wants to show him.* Cash my paycheck, tell it to Annetta, then onto the next assignment. The idea of anything more existed nowhere in my mind until that moment, and to this day, I don't know if I'm grateful or resentful of Malik for planting it there. While my brain worked over Malik's ideas, one notion leapt to the foreground. "Trap him? How the hell would we trap him?"

"Tranquilizers and Ketch-All poles. That's how we used to handle dangerous animals and meth heads." My blank look made Malik chuckle. "Let me tell you the difference between trying to subdue a wild animal, like an invading black bear or a potentially rabid dog, and a tweaker who laced his crystal with bath salts: give me a choice, I'll take the animal every time. Scared animals are dangerous but predictable. They'll try to get away from you until they can't, and then they attack. They don't really want to fight. They want you to go away and leave them alone. You can use that, get close enough to put a tranq dart in their posterior, or string a Ketch-all loop over their head. You know those things? Pole with a strong loop of wire at one end. You can control the size of the loop by adjusting the pole."

"Yeah, I've seen them in movies — but never used for a person. That seems cruel."

"Yeah, well, that's because you never had to face down a tweaker who'd gnawed halfway through his own left wrist and started screaming about eating your face the moment he saw you. Guys like that are so far out of their heads they're not even running on animal instinct anymore. They're pure madness with teeth and nails, trying to do to the body of anyone who comes too close what the drugs are doing to their mind. You remember that guy down in Florida years back caught buck naked at the side of the highway chewing the face off a hobo?"

"Uh, yeah, crazy stuff. Bath salts, right?"

"Right. I saw worse than that on the job. Spare you the gory details, but one dude... it took me and three other guys with Ketch-Alls to subdue him. We hit him with three tranqs. No effect. Whatever was in his blood was way stronger than the sedative. His girlfriend is still on the list for a face transplant."

"You're not exactly giving me a lot of confidence about our chances of capturing one of those things that way if it took four of you to bring down a single tweaker."

"Not things, Bigfoots. They're Bigfoots for sure so let's not pussyfoot around. Call them what they are. You missed my point. If there's any rationality to them, even the basest animal instinct, then one, we can trick them, and two, once they're looped, they focus on the pole, not the person holding it. All we have to do is tranq them, then shove them into a… a cage or something."

I tried to picture wrangling a Bigfoot while Malik aimed a tranq gun at him, but every scenario I imagined ended with me flung into the woods or slammed against a tree while our Bigfoot ran off with a pole hanging from his neck. A cage? Where the hell did one buy a cage big and strong enough to restrain an angry Bigfoot?

"I got it!" Malik said as if he'd read my mind. "We use a shark cage. I know a guy in Montauk who makes them for the shark charter boats. Strong as nails. They'll keep a twenty-foot Great White from making lunch out of anyone dumb enough to get into the water with them. I'll bet that'll do the job."

"Give me a minute here," I said.

I walked the yard again, eyeing the stomped-in prints. The power in those impressions, the brute strength hinted at by six-inch deep imprints in solid earth when the thing seemed like it only meant to scare us, gave me serious doubts about Malik's shark-cage proposal. It had taken me both hands and lifting with my legs to move the branch it had swung and thrown at us as if it weighed no more than a tooth-pick. The second creature's footprints gave me equal concern for the wisdom of Malik's plan. I imagined Malik and his colleagues getting that first tweaker under control when two more rushed them from out of nowhere. *How would that go?* I wondered. A flurry of unhappy face-eating, I suspected.

"Malik, I have to ask you a question," I said.

"Shoot," he said.

"I'm no cop. I don't even know any cops. I don't know, man, is shooting drugged-up suspects with tranquilizer darts considered proper police procedure?"

"Whatever keeps you alive is proper police procedure, hear me? That was a hell of a lot more humane than if we had to take them down physically. No question someone would wind up with broken bones and a wealth of bruises that way. If we bent the truth a little and reported the tranq gun had belonged to the perp, and he accidentally dosed himself while resisting, no one bothered to ask." Malik put his hand on my shoulder. "I know you're mulling over what exactly you'd be getting into here. Weighing if this is your big shot as a reporter or more likely to land you in the hospital. All I can say, Ben, is I didn't believe in any of this stuff until a few weeks ago. I still don't buy into any more of it than I've experienced, but you were there with me last night, and that is as real as it gets. Now you've got a choice, son. Take your story, go home, cash a check. Or stay for the *real* story and launch your whole damn career. So, you in or not?"

A Japanese beetle landed in one of the footprints, scrambled around like an elephant in the Grand Canyon, then flitted away. I imagined the foot that had made the print landing on the beetle, the bug vanishing in its shadow, depressed into the soil, and then I gave Malik my answer.

CHAPTER ELEVEN

I assumed obtaining a large enough shark cage would take days, if not weeks, but, no, incredibly, Malik's guy had one in stock. He had built it for the yacht of a Wall Street billionaire who never claimed it, afraid if he did, he'd only lose it in the midst of nasty divorce proceedings with his third wife. Malik made up a story about his nonexistent brother's fishing boat, and the guy agreed to sell it to him for a pittance to get it out of his workshop. People stared, wide-eyed and curious, as Malik drove us back to his place with the cage strapped into the bed of his truck. I felt like a special guest on an episode of Shark Week, but one of the cheesy ones where they try to convince you Megalodons have survived into the present. Lucky for us, Malik kept a tranquilizer pistol and handful of darts when he retired, so all we needed were more cameras and mics. I took the pickup to a security shop, then the nearest outdoors store to purchase the gear. I returned to find the shark cage positioned on the edge of the Barrens and disguised by a thick layer of branches and leaves. If you didn't know to look for it, you wouldn't see it right away.

The rest of the afternoon went to placing trail cameras and GoPros to cover the border between Malik's yard and the Barrens. Maybe $2,000 in gear, all purchased on Malik's credit card. Something told me not all of it would survive the night. I hoped he could afford it. Cashing in a favor from a local veterinarian, Malik purchased sedative for the tranq darts under the pretense of a bad raccoon problem and not wanting to drop a grand on pest control services for a job he could do himself. When it came to raccoons, suburban people like us cozied up to the idea of "re-homing" them rather than killing them, so the vet didn't ask too many questions. I wondered what Malik had done for him in the past to earn the favor.

That evening, Malik grilled again, and we ate outside. I showered and borrowed a clean T-shirt, feeling halfway human again without the stink of fear-sweat that had soaked into my other shirt constantly in my nose. We spoke little about the Bigfoots, keeping to small talk about the food and how Malik missed his wife and wanted to get this over with so she would come back home. I missed Annetta. We texted a few times to keep in touch, but her symposium kept her busy pretty much from morning to night. A summer week of nothing but talking science might seem deadly dull to some folks, but Annetta liked it better than a vacation, I think. That took more than professional interest. It took passion. I added that to the list of the many things I admired about her.

We finished off our meal at sundown then took up our positions.

After training me with the gun all afternoon, Malik put me in charge of tranquilizing Bigfoot. That brought me great relief, except now my imagination painted scenarios that all ended with Bigfoot flinging Malik into the woods before running off with the Ketch-All pole hanging from its neck.

I lay down in the truck bed with the tailgate down, the truck parked in the center of the yard, giving me a full view of the Barrens. Malik hid off to the side of the yard with the Ketch-All pole, posted where he could rush Bigfoot from the side, loop him, and use his momentum to keep the creature heading toward the open shark cage. Nothing about this plan gave me much confidence. Several times that day, I had pressed Malik to bring in more people to help, but he refused. *Who would believe us, and why would we want to share the greatest discovery of the century? We got this!* Each time I asked, he shut me down and back slapped me like a junior trainee questioning the mastery of his superior.

I set up my camera on its tripod. By the time the sun vanished below the horizon, Malik and I had each settled in and gone quiet.

After a couple of hours, I struggled to keep my eyes open. I hadn't slept at all the previous night, and the adrenalin and excitement that had sustained me through the day had dissipated. The humidity lessened, the night cooled, and the hard surface of the truck bed almost felt comfortable. I nodded off now and then until finally dipping into the Thermos of coffee Malik had prepared, sipping only enough for the caffeine to hit me, afraid to drink so much I'd have to take a leak.

Midnight passed. Then one a.m. Nothing stirred in the Barrens. I searched for Malik, but even knowing where he hid, I couldn't find him.

The trees and bushes around him remained perfectly still, and that gave me the first bit of hope that our plan might work.

Two a.m. brought knocking from the woods. Distant but unmistakable. Wood against wood. Echoing in its strange way among the trees, yet loud enough to make me tremble. A faraway howl followed. All the insect noise ceased then, all at once, like a signal from the emergency broadcast system silenced the night's regularly scheduled mating calls and buzz-click symphonies. No need for coffee to stay awake now. The knocks and howls did that fine, but no motion came to the Barrens. No vibrating thumps from massive, stamping feet. The Bigfoots kept their distance. Around 3:30 a.m., bushes to my right, near the shark cage, maybe thirty yards away, rattled with motion. I nearly cried out in shock, but then a deer appeared. Oblivious to my presence, it strolled across the yard and exited to the Barrens on the other side.

After another hour of knocks and howls, it occurred to me that Malik and I had never asked any of his neighbors if they heard them. I made a mental note to do so in the daytime. Soon the noise ended. Half an hour passed. The bug concert resumed. I gave in to sleep.

Malik shook me awake at dawn, a scowl on his face.

"No shows," he said.

Groggy, I sat up, my stiff muscles complaining, and swung my feet over the edge of the tailgate. "Think they're onto us?"

"You mean like they know what we have planned? No way. They just don't come every night. Told you that already. We'll give it another go tonight."

Another night at Malik's meant another email to Malachy to explain why I needed more time on the story. That could go either way. Annoyance that such a trivial piece caused him any inconvenience or indifference because such a lightweight article could run anytime. He came back with the latter.

I shared with Malik my idea about talking to his neighbors and then crashed on his couch. He let me sleep through until dinner before waking me up.

"You needed it," he said. "I want you sharp out there tonight."

Over another backyard dinner, Malik said, "Took your advice. Asked my neighbors. They thought I was joking. None of them have experienced anything like what we have. No shaggy monsters trying to beat down their backdoor, no weird footprints, no gargantuan piles of poop. No howls, no knocks."

I shrugged as I chewed a mouthful of barbecue chicken. "Maybe they're heavy sleepers?"

"That makes no sense. Those noises are so loud, they ought to have heard something."

"Maybe they sleep with air conditioners on, and it blocks out the sound."

"I guess. Maybe."

Malik dropped the subject, but I saw in his eyes how the information troubled him. Up until now, none of this seemed personal, only the result of chance that these creatures chose his yard to intrude, the same way the deer had randomly walked through it last night. But one deer meant others, and I bet if Malik had asked his same neighbors if they'd seen deer around, or deer scat, or found their gardens eaten by deer at times, they all would've said yes.

Taking our same positions, we staked out the yard again. Better rested, I stayed awake fine, but the previous night repeated itself. We caught only the faintest indications of activity, sounding more distant than they had before and that much farther out of our grasp. Not even a deer crossed our path. By morning, Malik fumed with anger, cursing the dumb things for staying away, comparing it to when you bring your car to the mechanic, and it runs fine even though it felt like it might fall apart on the drive to the garage. That didn't quite encapsulate it for me. Instead, looking into the indifferent Barrens gave me the same sensation as searching for the missing road to Ms. Sung's house. The aftermath of experiences intended for a specific time and place, things to be sensed, experienced, known but never recorded or shared, only possible when they caught you off guard, unprepared, as if offering insight and understanding for you alone, not the entire world strung together breathlessly awaiting the next viral sensation.

Malik asked me to stay another night. I considered it, but then a text from Annetta popped up in my notifications and convinced me the time had come to leave: *Coming home early. Ms. Sung called. Monty's coming back. Can you meet me tomorrow?*

Chapter Twelve

In a Brooklyn coffee shop, Annetta listened wide-eyed, a skeptical eyebrow raised, to the story of my efforts with Malik to catch the Bigfoots stalking his home. By then, I'd attributed at least some of what I'd experienced to my imagination, fueled by Malik's strong personality and conviction of the thing's reality. Buying into his story, I'd exaggerated ordinary noises from the Pine Barrens into secret Bigfoot code, and with some time passed, the footprints seemed smaller, less impressive and fantastic in my photographs than they'd seemed after a sleepless night. Many inexplicable things remained about my experiences at Malik's house, especially what exactly had chased us, but only because I hadn't found the explanation yet. By the time I finished the story, I'd mostly convinced myself of all this, and so Annetta's reaction caught me off guard.

After saying not a word for the duration of my tale, she beamed at me and said, "That is uh-*mazing*! You have to show me. I want to see it all, the footprints, everything. I want to meet Malik. It's incredible, truly incredible. I wish I could've been there."

"You believe me?" I said.

"You're not lying, Ben. You've got the pictures to prove it. Physical evidence at Malik's too. It's a genuine first, Bigfoot on Long Island. Did you file your story?"

I nodded. "Should post to the site by tomorrow. No idea what my editor will do with it."

Annetta laughed. "I can't believe you tried to catch Bigfoot in a shark cage."

The comedy of it struck me, and I laughed too.

"The good news is," Annetta said, "we're going to be heading back out to that neck of the woods. Ms. Sung figures the next visible passage of the Montauk Monsters will be tomorrow night. She sent me the location, and we're both going to be there. Assuming you're in, that is."

"Oh, hell yeah, I'm in, but are you sure Monty will be there?"

"Not at all. I'm taking Ms. Sung at her word and hoping this pays off, but nothing is ever a sure thing, you hear me? We keep at it, keep on trying until we find what we're looking for or decide it doesn't exist."

"You think it's safe?"

Annetta frowned, questioning. "Safe how?"

"To take Ms. Sung at her word after the way she seemed to vanish off the face of the Earth."

The shadow that came over Annetta's expression showed she hadn't considered any risk. Her excitement had overridden all other considerations. "I see your point. We'll be careful. No matter what, we can't pass up this opportunity."

We agreed Annetta would pick me up the next morning for the drive out east and then finished lunch. I invited her to hang around a while, maybe go to a park, but she had too much to prepare. I took the Long Island Railroad home. As I walked up my street from the train station, my insides froze despite the steamy July weather. A black car sat in my driveway. I didn't recognize it. Something about it felt... *off*. That's the only way I can describe it. A late-model, four-door sedan, but of no make or model I could place, as if it were comprised of parts plucked from similar cars produced by a variety of manufacturers. So many cars on the road shared the same basic body shape and chassis. I couldn't say exactly why it looked so odd. The tinted front windshield didn't help, nor the absence of a manufacturer's logo. Instead of glossy body paint, a dull, flat black with the albedo of primer covered it. As I walked up my driveway, heat radiated from the vehicle as if it absorbed energy from the high, bright sun. I held my palm an inch from the surface of the trunk, but caution stopped me from touching it, an instinctual fear of receiving a shock or leaving a mark — or lowering my hand and meeting no resistance at all, passing right through the surface, and I had no idea why that notion came to mind.

A loud thump from inside my house snapped my attention away from the car.

I walked around to the back door, eased my key into the lock then crept in without making a sound. Footsteps from the living room. A murmur. A voice? My radio playing with the volume dialed way down? I crept across my kitchen, and as I stepped into my tiny dining room, which opened onto the living room, a flurry of footsteps sounded, and the front door banged. I rushed into the living room. No one there. An old coat rack my parents left behind when they retired to Florida lay on its side. The door hung open. Outside, an engine purred. I ran and burst out onto the front stoop in time to see the black car gliding down my block, around the corner, and out of sight. No other word fit how it moved. As if the tires rode on a current of air two inches above the ground, it *glided*. It ran quiet, like an electric car, but with a mild crackling, hissing sound, like a downed power line popping and sparking.

As the car vanished, fear that someone had stayed behind made me jump around and look back inside, but the living room remained empty. I called the police and waited outside for them to come. They cleared my house, took my description of the car, and stayed while I checked my valuables, all still where they belonged, including my cameras and the memory cards that held my photos from the day with the Ms. Sung and the nights at Malik's. Nothing looked disturbed except that old coat rack. The cops promised to stay in touch, but I saw the case already closing in their eyes. *Trespassing, nothing more, not worth the time, but stay alert and let us know if you see the car again or anyone else comes creeping around, have a good day, citizen, and, hey, let's be careful out there.* Sure. I closed and locked the door behind them.

I called Ethan. A recorded message answered and said his cell phone was no longer in service. I tried Lana. Straight to voicemail. I left a message then tried her four more times, all answered by voicemail. I waited three hours, tried again. Voicemail. Finally, I called Annetta, who answered on the second ring, her sweet voice a lifeline. I didn't know what to think or say about my uninvited visitor, so I only confirmed our plans for the next day. I gathered my gear, set all my camera batteries to charge, and then contemplated sleep. A wall of fear stood between me and even the notion of crawling into bed and shutting off the lights. I sat up in my recliner with all the living room lights on until fatigue closed my eyes. Even then, my brain stayed alert for the creak of the door, for the hiss and snap of electricity from that mysterious car. I woke several times, each a false alarm, the neighbors slamming car doors, owls hooting, ordinary sounds, and then drifted through a restless sleep.

I awoke again to a knock at my door and daylight streaming through the windows.

CHAPTER THIRTEEN

Annetta teased me about oversleeping, but once I grabbed a quick shower and collected my gear, we hit the road only twenty minutes late. A sour haze hung over everything. The horizon looked gray and dirty, a stark difference from the last time we'd undertaken this drive. As if oppressed by the weather, traffic flowed at a sluggish pace. Even so, we made better time on a weekday than during the weekend rush and soon reached our destination, the diner near Montauk. Annetta treated me to lunch, and then we made our first stop of the day at Malik's house. I'd called ahead, so when we rolled up in Annetta's Prius, Malik sat waiting on the porch.

He eyed the car. "See you got yourself one of those putt-putt cars. They let you on the golf course with those things?"

"I wouldn't know. I don't play golf," Annetta said. "I can drive a month before I need to refill the gas tank, though, so I suppose I could afford to try."

"You catch a Bigfoot, how are you going to transport him in something like that?"

"Cross that bridge if I ever come to it." Annetta introduced herself and then shook hands with Malik.

Seeing a roguish, admiring gleam in his eyes, I said, "Hey, Mal, has the missus come back home yet?" I choked down a laugh at how fast his expression changed when he stepped back from Annetta.

"Still at her sister's place," he said, his tone gruff. "Anyway, you come on around back. I'll show you what's what."

We took our time, the heat of the day and the stifling humidity suppressing any urge to hurry. A film of sweat gathered on our foreheads. Behind Malik's house, the Pine Barrens stood shrouded in mist. Not the morning kind that burned off when the sun rose, but the kind where you can almost see individual droplets of moisture hanging in the air. Malik showed Annetta what remained of the footprints after a couple of days' exposure to the elements, the tire skids from his pickup, the sticks we'd collected, even the shark cage, at which she laughed in an impressed and awed way as she picked at its camouflage. While he gave her the tour, I photographed the woods, feeling sure the Barrens watched me with hidden eyes. Peel away the haze and mist, and it would reveal a secret audience. Observers studying me, Annetta, and Malik the same way we studied Monty and the signs Malik's Bigfoots left. Objects of fascination. Worlds separated by a veil, not quite solid or opaque nor quite thin and translucent. Oil on water, a rainbow film in the sun. A weird image to conjure at that moment, but that's what came. Then a shadow crossed among the trees. I lowered my camera for a better sense of its proximity but quickly raised it again because I couldn't see it without the aid of the lens. It moved through the haze but betrayed no sense of its size or shape, only its presence. The mist swallowed it. Then I saw nothing but trees and the gauzy, damp air.

"Anyone else feel like we're being watched?" I asked when I rejoined Annetta and Malik.

Annetta gave me a funny look, but Malik nodded. "All the time, son. Prying eyes are everywhere."

"Mind if we go inside then," I said. "I'm feeling, I don't know, exposed out here."

No one objected. The air conditioning in Malik's house offered welcome relief from the humidity. Malik put on a pot of coffee, and I checked to see if Malachy had posted my story yet. I found it cut down even worse than my Montauk Monster piece. It painted Malik as a quaint crackpot with an eccentric obsession. The text beside the photo of the camouflaged shark cage even dubbed him a "landlocked Quint," a reference to *Jaws* that only worked if you didn't think about it for more than a nanosecond. Nice job, Malachy. At least the check had cleared, and an email from Malachy in my inbox reported record clicks and views, even complimented my photos. Altogether a career "win," I guess, even if the story bent the truth out of any recognizable shape and dampened my celebration. I called Ethan to ask if he'd seen it, but his cell remained out of service, answered by a robovoice. Maybe, laid up and out of work, he hadn't paid his bill. No luck with Lana, either. Still straight to voicemail, but when I tried to leave a message, a recording declared her inbox full and disconnected me with an aggressive click.

"Hey, Malik, have you been in touch with Ethan and Lana recently?" I asked.

"No, but I haven't really tried. Pinged them on the message board a couple of times, but they've been offline, I guess," he said. "Maybe Ethan's feeling well enough they're holed up in their own little love cocoon, if you catch my drift. Anyway, you ready for another team-up?"

I dropped my phone on his coffee table. "No, man, I can't stand another night in your truck."

"Oh, no, not Bigfoot. I'm coming with you and Annetta. She told me where you're going tonight. It's off-limits after dark. Get caught there, you're gonna spend a night in jail, guaranteed. All the local cops have standing orders about this place. Zero tolerance for trespassers. Even the local teens steer clear of there, and there's pretty much no place they don't feel entitled to stamp all over. I can make a couple of calls, though, tell them you're friends of mine birding for some rare lunar dune warbler or whatever. Bring my badge and ID, so the officers on duty know who I am, and you get to look for Monty worry-free."

Having a retired sheriff along couldn't hurt, and having seen Malik in action, I knew it would help if we encountered any trouble. He even offered to drive us all out to Flamingo Avenue to see if we could find Ms. Sung's house. As we piled into his Tundra, he made a show of opening the door for Annetta and helping her in. I couldn't say if he meant to flirt or if he simply played the part of the chivalrous lawman with all women. Whatever the answer, I blushed when Annetta turned to me, seated in the back, winked, and blew me a kiss. The unexpected gesture set off all sorts of mixed signals in my brain, far too confusing to interpret then and there, so I smiled, winked, and played it cool—except now I regretted having Malik along, stopping me from discovering if more than playfulness lay behind that wink.

We cruised Flamingo Avenue several times, focused on a strip of blacktop between Wills Point Road and Blackberry Drive, but found no sign of the turnoff, no houses, nothing but lush green summer brush, and other cars zipping past us. Malik parked on the shoulder. For half an hour, we walked up and down, ventured into the wooded areas, and still found nothing. Back at the truck, as we brushed ticks off our clothes and checked our legs and arms for them, we lapsed into a baffled and defeated silence. Malik opened one of the locked compartments in his truck bed and returned with a drone cradled in his arms.

"Only one other way to see if we can find this place," he said as the drone buzzed into the air.

He controlled it with finesse. It lifted straight up, hovered overhead, then soared high above the area to the west of us. Annetta and I gathered around Malik and watched the video screen on his controller. Nothing but trees, brush, birds, and bugs. The Long Island Sound gleamed blue-white in the distance. After fifteen minutes, he piloted the drone over the wild land to our east. Another fifteen minutes of nothing. Malik guided the device back and landed it at his feet.

"I'll have to recharge the battery if you want to keep looking," he said.

"I don't get it. A house can't just disappear," I said.

Annetta dialed a number on her cell phone and held it to her ear. She lowered it, swiped the screen, and then dialed again and listened.

"Who are you calling?" I asked.

Lowering the phone, she said, "Ms. Sung. No answer. She never gave me a number. I'm dialing back the number she used to call me."

"It's possible we're on the wrong road. We used GPS to find the place the second time. It's not always right. One time I followed it getting onto the Seaford-Oyster Bay Expressway and wound up in a strip mall," I said.

"Tell you what, I'll put in some calls, see if any of my contacts know Ms. Sung, ask them to check out the address," Malik said. "If they're out here, at least one of the local cops will know who they are."

As we drove away, I watched the wild stretch give way to downtown and houses at the side of the road, side streets leading off to residential areas. A twinge at the back of my neck set my hair on edge. I twisted around and gazed out the rear window. Behind us, a black car cut a sharp right and vanished down a side street. I didn't see it long enough or clear enough to say why, but I felt sure the same car had sat in my driveway that day someone invaded my house. I almost asked Malik to turn around and follow it, but black cars aren't uncommon, and I'd only glimpsed it.

From the world of houses and stores, the wild patch looked small and unremarkable, land neglected because the ground didn't suit building, or some environmental concern shielded it. How strange that such a small distance made such a big difference, that the border between safe, familiar surroundings and untouched land stretched so thin, so easy to cross, and yet looking at one from the other offered startlingly different views. A shadow crossed the sun. A raft of gray clouds passed quickly and soon lost its shape. Then it all fell out of sight, leaving a tingling at the base of my skull.

CHAPTER FOURTEEN

Two things stood east of Ditch Plains Beach. Beach-side wilderness and the Atlantic Ocean. Although "wilderness" seemed inaccurate. Park boundaries contained all that land, and the largest park, Camp Hero, once served as a Cold War radar station. It still contained remnants of the military installation, including a massive radar antenna mounted atop one of the buildings. At the very tip of the land's end, on the pointed tine of one of Long Island's two forks, stood the Montauk Lighthouse. A popular landmark and tourist stop. Even after all I'd experienced with Annetta and Malik, the presence of an unknown, undiscovered animal on this well-trod ground strained probability. Maybe in the Pine Barrens, which stretched and rambled over a patchwork of land, but not here, not where roads so intercut the woods, and people visited all year round. But then, I'd never set foot in such a place after the sun fell below the horizon.

Night changed everything. Cars stopped coming, and no one walked or biked the trails. Trees that stood apart, individual, in the daylight, blended together in the dark, masses of shadowed leaves and branches like newborn mountain ranges. Stars filled the cloudless sky. The night surf licked the beach, the tongue of a leviathan stretched beyond the black edge of the sea. Lights on faraway boats resembled bugs on the back of the beast. Parasites. Ticks. That nightfall alteration transformed the world again into one of maybes, and what-ifs, and secrets—and then Malik, maybe bored by sitting on the beach and watching blank water, threw utterly out of whack the delicate balance I'd struck among my desire to spend time with Annetta, my simultaneously growing skepticism of and interest in cryptozoology, and my desire to sleep at home in my well-worn bed, with one simple sentence.

"You heard about the experiments the government did on children here, right?"

Annetta lowered the night-vision binoculars she held aimed out to sea and shushed him. I straightened in one of the beach chairs Malik had brought for us. "Say what now?"

"Yeah, real Cold War stuff, right after WW II. Underground, under cover of this radar base. I mean, you know that part, right? Everyone does. The government acknowledges that. Got the whole history of this place documented as part of the early warning and response system for nuclear or other attacks by air or submarine. They camouflaged this place as a fishing village to conceal the barracks and built the gun emplacements into the ground. We passed all that coming in, that decrepit radar antenna, right? But what no one admits to is running psych warfare research here, experiments to open access to other dimensions, to time travel, to psychic spying. You heard of the Philadelphia Experiment in '43? Navy tried to make a destroyer escort invisible and wound up sending it through time or into another dimension or something? The work for that started here, and it involved children."

"Okay, wait, there's a movie about that one with the missing ship, right?" I said.

Malik nodded. "Try to find real government records of it, though, and good luck."

"They don't exist because it never happened," Annetta said. "Now, will you be quiet and focus on what we came here for? Patricia said when the Monties come through, they won't be visible for long. I don't want to miss them. You sure you got your camera set correctly, Ben?"

To ease Annetta's mind, I checked the low-light and night settings on my camera and the trail cameras from our Bigfoot hunt. If anything interesting passed within range, the video would show it. Patricia claimed the things stayed close to shore when they surfaced. They liked the shallows, or the land's magnetic field, something like that, she'd told Annetta. It made as much sense as any of the rest of this plan did.

In a voice barely above a whisper, Malik said, "They kidnapped Long Island kids, street kids, neglected kids, delinquents whose parents wouldn't notice them missing overnight or for a couple of days. It had to be kids, see, because their brains aren't fully formed. The experiments reshaped the folds of their gray matter, rewired them so they saw things invisible to ordinary eyes. Getting to a destination, being able to see it is half the battle. So, the story goes, once these kids saw outside our dimension, or through time, or on some wavelength no ordinary human could see, they opened the way to other worlds. So, the military brought the best ones back again and again, trying to find a way to weaponize what they could do."

"Come on, Malik. You expect me to believe this? Didn't they make a television show about this? Kids and another dimension?" I whispered to avoid censure from Annetta.

"Yes, they did, and no, I don't," Malik said. "I didn't say I believed it, son. It's a conspiracy theory, that's all, and we're sitting right on top of the inspiration for it. I'm just passing the time. Figured you might use it for some color in your next story."

I had no next story at the moment. Despite Malachy's compliments and the success of my photo features, no new assignment had come my way, no offer of staff employment. Tough economic times, shrinking markets for traditional news platforms, competition from social media all explained well enough why I found myself jobless for the moment, but I couldn't help thinking my stories had more to do with it. I'd made a lot of work for Malachy to cut them up. Maybe he took me for a weirdo because I'd written about them in all seriousness. The online world didn't work that way. Readers expected articles to mock things they found silly or didn't like. Snark ruled. Opinions counted more than facts. If you didn't look down your nose at anything that fell outside "accepted reality" in the online world, you were naïve, or ignorant, or ill-informed, or, worse, shooting marbles from a mostly empty bag. I didn't feel like getting into it with Malik, so I offered only an indifferent, "Maybe."

He took that as encouragement. "You should share your byline with me, I bring you so many good stories. Now, these Camp Hero experiments, they weren't the only ones the government ran like that. There was MK Ultra, too. Research into brainwashing and mind control. And Project Stargate, where they investigated remote viewing. Some folks call it clairvoyance or clairaudience. The ability to see or hear things on the other side of the world. Both of those are real, documented programs the government spent money on. All to win the Cold War. Maybe they were just elaborate psyops, programs intended to make the Soviets think we could do those things, so they'd worry and waste their own time trying to match us. Or vice-versa. Who the hell knows? I wouldn't be surprised if even the folks who ran those programs didn't know. But if those happened, then why not Camp Hero? You think a government willing to secretly infect 600 Tuskegee sharecroppers to study the effects of syphilis or release flu virus in a New York City subway tunnel to track its spread—both things we *know* happened— you think that government would draw the line at abducting a few poor kids?"

"Geez, Malik, listen to you go on," Annetta said. "I thought you didn't believe in any of this stuff."

"I *said* I don't. Or at least I *didn't* a month ago. Then Bigfoot started taking dumps in my backyard, and now I'm questioning everything I know about how the world works."

The statement hung in the air for a moment before all three of us burst with laughter. Annetta laughed the loudest. It took a few minutes for it to die down, for us to catch our breath and return to calmness, but when we did, it lasted only a moment.

In the lull that followed, the water beyond the low, endlessly rolling breakers erupted with splashes as something thrashed to the surface. Annetta raised her binoculars and adjusted the night vision settings. I knelt beside my camera on its tripod, the screen capturing only movement and the glint of starlight on water until I fiddled with the focus and the settings, rendering the image with additional clarity. Annetta and I gasped, almost in unison.

"What is it? What do you see?" Malik rushed to the edge of the surf, trying to see with the naked eye what our lenses revealed. The thrashing neared the shore, improving our view, and then Malik saw what we saw. "Oh, dear god, is that… a shark?"

Chapter Fifteen

My wildest expectations for what we might see had extended as far as a school of fish that jumped at night or baby otters at play, both normal, explicable, and easily mistaken for something else by casual observers in darkness. What frothed the water was no school of fish or mischievous otters.

Two dozen Montauk Monsters—I don't know what else to call them—swarmed what the three of us later decided was a young Great White, about eight feet long. A burst of motion, wet fur, cleaver-like beaks, and white teeth surrounded the gray fins of the dying beast. Its gills throbbed. Its mouth opened and closed, exposing triangles of razor-sharp teeth that did nothing to protect it. An apex predator, the shark had almost no defensive anatomy. Built to swim, to strike, to devour, it succumbed to the mass of creatures chewing its body and fins. The Montauk Monsters moved too fast to afford us a good look at them, but they created an impression not unlike otters or beavers or any other furry mammal at home in the water. Except they fed like piranhas, relying on their numbers, swiftness, and determination to take down their prey and devour it.

An emerald luminescence with no obvious source lit the scene. It imbued the water with hazy brightness, shimmered on the Montauk Monsters' fur, cast light on the shark's blood staining the water red. No blood stuck to the Monsters. It rolled off them into the water. I adjusted my camera to account for the light, wondering if it came from some bioluminescent algae or plankton. Its brightness ebbed and flowed, and I worked the camera to keep up with it. Annetta and Malik stood transfixed by the sight. If I hadn't been so determined to capture good video for Annetta, I might've found myself too amazed to act. Whatever we witnessed then, I held not a shred of doubt that almost no one else on earth had seen such a sight. That nature, or the cosmos, or a higher being had granted us something special that night. I kept that notion at bay, though, frightened it might overwhelm me and leave me helpless. Every nerve in my body fired, every hair stood on end, goosebumps appeared on my flesh, and my senses raced to keep up with the stimuli. A terrible odor drifted on the air, not a low-tide stench, worse, one I knew from another night spent playing the Bigfoot-hunting game. My brain couldn't process its presence, but I knew the stink meant we weren't alone. Bigfoot lurked nearby.

The glow around the Montauk Monsters flared. Ripples of light, like a reflection of the Aurora Borealis on the water's surface, shimmered with an array of colors that burned firework flashes across my eyes. The light emanated from the Monsters' fur. Then half of them vanished, submerged, or swam away, but, no, I hadn't seen that. They had been there one second, gone the next with the dying pulse of light.

Annetta's voice pierced the spell we'd all fallen under. "Where the hell did they go?"

She rushed down the beach, into the surf, her night vision binoculars held firm against her eyes. Another pulse of light built up around the remaining Monsters and their meal. It rippled off their fur in curling waves like green smoke. Annetta waded in up to her knees, oblivious to the water rising around her. Terrified of what they might do to her, of the thrashing shark biting her, or what could happen if she stood too close when this light pulse peaked then flickered out, I called her back, then chased her. Water splashed my legs. Energy coursed through it, like ozone in the air after a thunderstorm. It lapped at me with an uncomfortable, prickling sensation. I reached Annetta and dragged her back to the beach. We fell together on the sand, recovering in time to see the glow flare then fade, taking the last of the Montauk Monsters with it. The shark, dead now, bobbed on the water, then jerked as something hit it from below. An unseen scavenger dragged it out to sea, then underwater and out of sight.

Stillness followed, abrupt and brittle. It lasted seconds before rustling stirred the beach grass and nearby brush. Dozens of pairs of eyes shimmering with starlight surrounded us and inched closer, tightening a semi-circle on the patch of sand we'd staked out for the night. Soft, barking noises passed among them, interrupted by high-pitched chittering, wheezes, and whimpers. I tightened my hold on Annetta, pushed myself in front of her. Still, when more Montauk

Monsters swarmed us, she screamed. So did I. So did Malik. Too numerous to count, a wriggling, rushing mass of chromatic fur, beaks, teeth, and claws rushed us, flowed around us, and plunged into the surf.

Rainbow shimmers coruscated in their fur. Their touch sparked as they brushed against one another, electric flashes, static shocks of emerald, ruby, citrine. They poured out from the darkness, a seemingly infinite column. Then, as quickly as it began, it ended. The water churned. Deep beneath the surface, a rich green borealis flared, providing a fleeting glimpse of the things swimming downward, a massive school of them, diving into the green aurora, vanishing, until none remained.

I don't know how much time passed while we sat there on the beach, stunned. Malik didn't move. He stared at the water. I should've felt terrified by what we'd seen, by my proximity to the surf, where the Monsters could return at any moment. I didn't. I couldn't explain how I knew it, but I knew they'd gone and would not come back. Events would not repeat tonight, maybe not for many nights to come. We had witnessed a special phenomenon. I had no room for fear. Elation filled me.

I helped Annetta to her knees. Unable to control my grin, trembling with excitement, I brushed sand from her face. "Are you all right?"

Our gazes met. With tears in her eyes, she mirrored my elation, then unleashed a wild, triumphant cry into the night. She grabbed me, hugged me, let go, jumped into the air.

"We saw them!"

So we had. A creature that shouldn't exist. A legend birthed from the supposed carcass of a dead raccoon.

We had discovered the truth. Then the first question tainted my excitement. Exactly what truth had we discovered? My mood sank, but I kept up appearances for Annetta's sake until I saw uncertainty creep into her expression, then into Malik's. We all faced the same dilemma: making sense of what we'd seen.

We sat vigil the rest of the night. The Monsters didn't reappear, but now and then, a dim knocking came from the trees between us and the road. The clack of wood against wood. And a rotten smell drifted by, then faded, only to return when the wind shifted a certain way. We were not the only ones who'd kept watch for the Montauk Monsters that night.

At dawn, I shot photos of the sunrise, of the remnants of small footprints in the sand as surf and wind erased them, and then we packed up and left. Malik's truck waited outside the gates on Camp Hero Road where he'd parked it the night before with a note in the window for any suspicious cops to call his cell. As we pulled out of the park onto Montauk Highway, a sight maybe a quarter mile down the road sent ice through my veins. A black car sat on the shoulder. The only other vehicle in sight until two cars rolled along, full of early beachgoers. Annetta and Malik knew about the intruder in my home, so when we settled into Malik's truck, I pointed out the car.

We couldn't avoid passing it on our drive home, so Malik stopped right beside it for a closer look. The tinted windows hid anyone inside. The car bore no manufacturer's logo, no identification except for license plates in a gold-on-black style New York State had abandoned decades ago. I rolled down my window to snap pictures of it and smelled the acrid, hot sawdust odor of an electrical fire. Malik opened his door to get out.

"No, don't mess with it," I said.

"Not going to mess with it, just check it out."

"Don't. It's not safe," I said.

Annetta leaned forward from the backseat. "What do you mean?"

"We should keep going. Okay? Ignore it."

I couldn't explain why, but I sensed we'd pressed our luck as far as we should at that moment. Whoever drove that black car, we'd caught them, called them out, and if we prodded them any further, we'd only force them to act.

My heart sank when Malik scowled at me, said, "Nonsense, man. If this is the guy who broke into your house, and now he's following us, he's the one who should be worried about his safety."

He stepped out of the truck then walked to the black car, approaching from behind, studying it, keeping his distance at first before he strode up to the driver's side window and rapped on the glass. Horrifying seconds passed while I wrestled to put a name to what frightened me so much about that car, about its presence — then the driver's side window lowered. Darkness inside. Malik leaned down to see the driver. I stopped breathing, raised my camera to my eye, and took pictures, the only way I knew to cope with the anxious ache spreading out from my gut to the rest of my body. A flash of movement inside. A glimpse of a pale chin and nose. Thin, white lips moving, speaking low, and then Malik snapped upright and stepped back from the car. The window rose. Malik returned to the Tundra and, without a word, put it in drive and pulled onto the road.

"Who was he? What did he say?" Annetta asked.

Good that she did, too, because I couldn't bring myself to voice the questions. Part of me didn't want to know. But Malik didn't answer. He drove in silence, eyes straight ahead, speed dead on the limit. The black car pulled onto the road and followed us, visible in the rearview mirrors. It stayed with us all the way back to Malik's, then drove on past the house and out of sight when Malik pulled into his driveway. A car in front of us, blocking in Annetta's Prius, forced Malik to stop short. Its presence gave me a moment of terror until Malik said, "That's Janae's car. Guess her sister got to be more annoying than Bigfoot."

Annetta and I had time to exchange one quick, worried look before Janae appeared at the front door and called out, "Malik! Where the hell you been all night? I've been worried sick."

"Honey," Malik said, stepping from his truck. "Meet some friends of mine."

Janae flashed Annetta a challenging look, her face like a floodgate restraining a torrent, one eyebrow raised in an unspoken question, until, as if knowing the perfect answer, Annetta slid her arm around me and pulled me against her. That seemed to satisfy some unspoken accusation for Janae, and it pleased me. As Malik introduced us, Janae smiled and invited us in for coffee. On the way in, Malik whispered to keep quiet about our monster hunt to avoid freaking out his wife. But while she put on a pot of coffee, in a quiet, steady voice that somehow resonated like approaching thunder, Janae said, "Mal, I expect you're going to have one hell of a good reason for why we have a shark cage in our backyard, and, pudding, I can't wait to hear it."

CHAPTER SIXTEEN

"Tell me something, Annetta. What exactly do we do with this now?"

We watched the video from Camp Hero for a third time while fueling up at a gas station by the Expressway on-ramp. Although dark and murky at times, it caught the glow in the water, with several scenes showing excellent views of the Montauk Monsters and their physiognomy.

"It's not enough, not on its own," Annetta said. "We need physical proof, samples, anything to show beyond question that Monty is an animal we've never cataloged."

"You don't think it's convincing on its own?" I said.

Annetta considered it while she paid the station attendant, then pulled out, accelerated up the ramp and onto the Expressway. Twilight settled into the sky, a beautiful display of shadow and color as we drove through the Pine Barrens. A display more ominous than pleasant to me now. After we'd returned to Malik's that morning, Janae had insisted we stay for the day and rest before driving home after our all-nighter, even whipping up a feast of grilled steak, salad, and cornbread to send us off on full stomachs. Malik had offered her the birdwatching cover story to explain our overnight at the beach, and she'd accepted it with obvious skepticism. Likewise, his claim he intended to turn the shark cage into a deer blind for hunting, at which she'd laughed out loud. A pleasant day, all things considered, but it felt good to head home.

"The video alone won't suffice. Not to any scientist or skeptic. At best, a scientist will find it interesting, maybe worth some follow-up investigation, but it's not proof. A skeptic will label it a fake, a clever CGI effect, and compare it to alien autopsy footage and Dr. Wilson's Nessie photo. And those who believe it will be the worst. They'll descend on that beach *en masse* to search for the Monsters. If we take Patricia Sung at her word, that will only drive them away and ruin our chances of seeing them again."

"I don't think we will," I said.

"Will what?"

"See them again. At least not that way. That felt like a once-in-a-life-time experience. Like they knew we wanted to see them, maybe even heard it from Patricia Sung, so they showed themselves to us — but *only* us. All we can do with this video and our story is give cryptozoology another massive question mark. I don't know about you, Annetta, but I'm not sure I want to do that. I don't want our names associated with a thing people mock or a story that others latch onto and maybe, I don't know, derail their lives to pursue."

Annetta didn't answer me for almost fifteen minutes before she said, "We keep the video under wraps until we gather more proof. I think we'll see them again. They revealed themselves to us like they revealed themselves to Patricia Sung. Now we know about them. They know we know. They can't ignore us, and — dear God in heaven, listen to me talk, to *us* talk, about these... animals as if they're intelligent and can communicate with people, like Patricia Sung is some cryptid Doctor Doolittle. My God, Ben, I'm so far off the beaten trail right now that if any of my colleagues heard me, they'd send me to Bellevue for a psych eval."

This time, I let the silence hang between us. The thought had crossed my mind that we were taking far too much on faith, falling deeper and deeper down a rabbit hole with no bottom. We couldn't explain Patricia Sung's disappearing house or Malik's behavior after speaking to the driver of the black car. He had refused to discuss it, acted like he didn't know what we were talking about, as if we had seen no black car, no driver, and when I showed him the pictures I'd taken of it, he laughed them off and changed the subject. Although Annetta focused on the Montauk Monsters, my gut connected them to the Bigfoots in the Pine Barrens. They had sought out Malik like Ms. Sung had sought Annetta. That made me the wild card in all this, the random factor introduced by chance after Ethan's accident.

On a hunch, I rang him on my cell and found his phone still offline, then tried Lana and bounced straight to her full voicemail. "Listen," I said to Annetta, "I know it's getting late, but let's swing by Ethan's place. I haven't been able to reach him or his girlfriend for days now. I'm worried. If he's home, we can ask him what he thinks about the video."

"You want to show it to them?"

"Maybe. Let's see how it goes."

"You think we can count on Malik to keep quiet about it?"

"Yeah, I trust him."

"I still want to know what the dude in the black car said to him."

"Me too, Annetta, me too," I said.

Forty-five minutes later, we pulled off the Expressway and headed for Ethan's house in Plainview. When we arrived, we found it dark, with no cars in the driveway, which seemed odd because Ethan couldn't drive until his cast came off, still a couple of weeks away. Annetta parked at the curb. We approached the front door, and I rang the bell. No one answered. I rang it again, then knocked, hoping for a light to spring to life inside. None did. I knocked harder, pounded, called Ethan's name, asked if he was okay, begged him to open up, but he didn't answer. The door remained shut tight.

"How well do you know Ethan?" Annetta said.

"Well enough he wouldn't move without telling me. This feels really wrong, Annetta. I'm worried."

"Let's look around back," she said.

The house showed no more signs of life from the backyard. I opened Ethan's detached garage in hopes of finding his car, but it stood empty except for rusty yard tools. I banged on the back door, peered through the window, then walked to the kitchen window and looked in on a dark and empty room. Ethan kept a spare key hidden in a flower box alongside his garage, inside a hollowed-out brick. I found it then used it to unlock and open the back door. As I entered, the house felt dead. I knew I wouldn't find Ethan or Lana here. Still, I searched, and with Annetta's help, looked into each and every empty room and cleaned-out closet, checked the cellar and the little attic space accessed by a hatch in the upstairs hallway. Nothing, no sign of Ethan, that he'd ever lived here, so thoroughly moved out that for a moment, I questioned if we were in the right house, but a telltale stain on the living room carpet confirmed it. I had been here the night Lana spilled her red wine.

I used my phone to surf Lana's online forum. Still active, with posts from less than an hour ago, but none from Ethan or Lana, not for days.

"They're gone," I said. "How can two people simply vanish into thin air with all their belongings?"

Annetta held my hand. "They didn't, Ethan. They just moved, picked up stakes, went somewhere else, that's all. I'm sure, wherever they are, they're fine. Maybe they wanted a new start. Or a family crisis came up. Or, hell, I don't know, Lana owes her bookie more dough than she can ever hope to pay and split town to avoid some goon breaking her legs for interest."

I gave Annetta the side-eye for that. "They're not on the run from some knuckle-duster, but what if something else came for them? What if the guy in the black car came here too? It was a black car that caused Ethan's crash. What if it was the same black car that started everything?"

Annetta made no attempt to answer me. I appreciated that. Guesses only fueled fear and worry. We locked up and left the house as we'd found it, then Annetta drove me home.

She helped carry my gear inside, and when I turned to say good night, she pulled me into her arms and kissed me softly on the lips. I didn't know what had brought us closer, sharing the excitement of the past night, the bond of a secret experience, or maybe—and I hoped this counted for at least part of it—maybe she simply felt about me the way I felt about her. Whatever the reason, when she asked to spend the night, I welcomed it, kissed her back, and led her to my bedroom, all thoughts of monsters and black cars, missing friends and strange behavior vanquished, thankfully, for a while, clearing space for the deep and utterly human connection I desperately needed.

CHAPTER SEVENTEEN

I spent a few days searching for Ethan online and around town at places I knew he frequented. I even called Malachy, but our editor hadn't been in touch with Ethan, who'd blown off several weeks of copy-editing assignments while laid up with his leg. He asked me to let him know if I found him so he could send him his severance check. I could use some money myself and almost asked Malachy for an assignment but thought better of it after hearing the anger in his voice. I drove by Ethan's house again and found it unchanged. I would've driven by Lana's too if I knew where she lived, but she had no address I could find and little online presence outside her forum, so odd in the era of social media. The forum remained as lively as ever. Threads even appeared asking about Ethan and Lana, missing them, hoping they were okay. I checked it daily, hoping for them to surface, and reply, to explain they'd gone off on an expedition to find some cryptid or other. They never did, and the summer continued, hot and slow.

By early August, Annetta and I saw each other every day and spent every night at her place in Brooklyn or mine on the Island. Our relationship moved past talk of Monty and other cryptids and flourished into a thing of its own, although we kept our ears open, even watched the video sometimes. After a few weeks of feeling blue without the thrill of investigating Bigfoots and Montauk Monsters, I didn't think very much about it. Annetta alone mattered to me. The way her body fit against mine when I put my arm around her as we walked down the Coney Island Boardwalk and she ate cotton candy. The scent of her lingering on my shirt after an embrace. The sound of her voice. The warmth of her fingertips. Her laugh. How her eyes lit up when she saw me. That meant more to me than anything else I'd taken away from the unreal sequence of events that commenced when I met her. I only hoped she saw the same light in my eyes when I looked at her. I surely felt it.

Both of us worried about what the end of summer might bring. When Annetta returned to teaching, her schedule would change, and I still needed steady employment. I'd picked up some gigs here and there, shooting for local news websites, and once for an architecture magazine that kept me in Manhattan for two days, but work came slow and far between.

Malik kept in touch, mostly via email, updating us about his Bigfoot problem. Things calmed after that night at the beach in Camp Hero Park. He still smelled them some nights, heard wood knocking in the Barrens, but they never approached his house again, and most nights, he slept clear through without disturbance. He emailed pictures of the shark cage, which Janae had commandeered as a trestle for her roses, adding a wrought iron bench inside, turning it into a garden curiosity that proved so popular with their neighbors they thought about getting their own cages. The local paper even did a photo piece about it — and I wished I'd somehow landed even that paltry assignment. More than the work, I wanted to see Malik again. I missed roaming around the East End. Missed the excitement and anticipation. Spending time with Annetta more than made up for it, though.

With Labor Day and the official end of summer on the horizon, all that we'd experienced seemed to me like a summer movie, a teenage vacation romance, a month-long neighborhood game of Manhunt — a thing real and eternal in the youthful moment of its occurrence, but one with an inevitable expiration date. One you could never go back to. Then two things happened to change my mind.

On a photoshoot for *The Brooklyn Eagle*, a job Annetta had helped me land through a friend, I saw the black car parked down the block from the restaurant featured in the assignment. The moment I noticed it with the tinted, driver's side window lowered halfway, a pale hand extending from a black sleeve hanging out of it, the hand withdrew, and the window rose shut, a message to me that the driver knew I'd noticed him and wanted to convey that to me to put me on alert for some unfathomable reason. The car pulled out and slid away with the traffic, its old-fashioned license plates gleaming in the sun while its body looked dull as asphalt.

Two days later, Malik emailed me a picture of a six-foot branch, two inches thick and stripped of bark, sticking out of his broken kitchen window. *Guess who came back,* the message on my phone screen read. *Janae went to her sister's again, and I could use your help.* The email arrived while Annetta was out jogging. I debated for half an hour before she returned whether to show it to her. I wanted to help Malik. I wanted to go back there, pick up the game where we'd left off, keep this spectacular summer going, dig for the answers that still eluded us — but not if any of that came between Annetta and me. She meant more to me than anything waiting out there in the shadows. My fingertip hovered over the delete icon, but then I put my phone down. Annetta needed to see the message and decide for herself if she wanted any part of it. If she did, I'd be there beside her. And if she didn't, well, Malik would be on his own. I'd ride out summer in Brooklyn, hot town, back of my neck getting dirty and gritty.

When Annetta came home, smiling and sweaty from her run, she knew by my expression something had come up. I showed her the email. She skimmed it, studied the picture. I tried to read her face. She made it easy. She grinned. She reached to hug me, but I retreated. "Whoa, you're a little sweaty there, Betty. Maybe hit the shower before you give me that hug."

She laughed. "I told you it wasn't over, wasn't a one-time thing. They're back."

"Don't jump to conclusions. There's a hundred ways that stick could've wound up in Malik's window." Annetta took my hand and walked me across the room toward the bathroom. "Wouldn't surprise me if Janae did it herself for an excuse to get a break from Malik."

"Is that how you think, Ben? Is that what I can expect if you ever need a break from me? A stick through my kitchen window?"

"Of course not. Your kitchen doesn't have a window."

She wrinkled her face. "Smartass."

She started the water in the shower, and then, with a wild look in her eye, grabbed me in a hot, sweaty embrace, planted her lips on mine, then pulled back and said, "Now you're a sweaty mess, too. Guess you'll have to hit the shower with me."

CHAPTER EIGHTEEN

Malik left the branch in place to show us.

He yanked off a vinyl tarp he'd thrown over it to cover the break in the glass. Maybe six feet long and stripped of bark, it had struck the glass like a javelin with enough speed to punch a hole through without shattering the entire pane. Like a bullet. Or pictures I'd seen of branches embedded in buildings or tree trunks in the aftermath of a hurricane.

Once I'd photographed the branch from inside and out, I helped Malik remove it, hefting the weight of it, far too much for Malik or me to throw with such force on our own. Either a catapult had sent that branch into Malik's kitchen, or a thing with incredible strength, a Bigfoot.

"Four nights ago, after things being so quiet for weeks, the knocking started again in the woods," Malik told us. "I recorded some of it if you want to hear. They kept their distance, though. Janae slept through it, thankfully. A couple of times, I walked outside in the middle of the night to listen and watch, and I heard them, but that's it. Didn't see them or smell them. Only heard that knocking. In the morning, I found no footprints or other signs they'd come anywhere near the house. Then the other night, little after 3 a.m., *wham-crash*, this branch sails through my window. *That* woke up Janae. I told her to stay low in the bedroom while I checked it out. Soon as I saw this thing with its bark peeled off, I knew it was them. Still didn't prepare me for what I saw outside."

Dense gray rainclouds brought a steady drizzle. Thunder boomed from far away. A chill hung in the air. One of summer's cold, dark days, custom made to ruin plans for beach and pool alike and send droves to malls and movie theaters.

"I better show you what I found before this rain picks up," Malik said.

We followed him to another tarp, weighed down with bricks, stretched across several small shapes in the backyard.

"That night, I looked past the branch, looked out here, I saw three of those hairy creeps, standing in my yard. They'd brought me… a gift, I guess, a token, a sign, maybe a warning? Who knows? I sure don't. They brought me this."

He kicked two bricks aside and then flipped away the tarp. The stench of decomposing flesh billowed out, and a cloud of flies scattered for a moment before settling back upon their meal. Annetta and I recoiled from the odor, covered our mouths and noses with our hands.

Three skinned Montauk Monsters lay on the earth in little pools of drying blood. Tied together on a stick jammed upright into the earth, their hides draped beside them. Their flesh glistened, soft and oily. An image flashed through my mind. Bigfoot ripping the hide from the bodies in one powerful yank of its mighty hand the way a trapper skinned a rabbit.

It took me a moment to regain my composure, to think to lift my camera and shoot pictures. I couldn't look straight at the hides, though, only from the corner of my eyes. How the light played across them, making them ripple with color, with energy, made them both painful and mesmerizing, a trap from which instinct protected me.

"For the first time this whole crazy summer, I experienced terror," Malik said. "Fear? Yeah. That night they came at us in my truck, they scared the hell out of me. Watching those things feast on a shark sent a chill down my spine. I've been scared, shocked, surprised, and amazed. This was different. I didn't have control of myself. I walked up to those things, as close as we are now, stepped into the thick of their awful stink even though I wanted to run inside and grab my gun. It wasn't courage. They made me do it. Made me tilt my head back to meet their gaze, and when I looked into their eyes, it was like looking into a clear winter night sky in the wilderness as far from light pollution as you can get. It was like seeing another world inside them or through them, another universe. Sparks of metallic color danced on their hair. Colors within colors. Shimmery. Liquid. Like a film."

"Like sunlight hitting oil on water," I said, an image that had come to my mind that first day at Malik's.

"Yeah, that's right. I lost my sense of time. My body moved how they wanted me to, my eyes saw what they wanted to show me, and it filled me up with… terror. No other word for it."

The constant drizzle swelled to a light rain, slicking us wet, but none of us moved to return inside. I feared Malik would stop talking if we broke the spell.

"You think they meant to threaten you?" I asked.

Malik shook his head. "That's the thing. It wasn't them that terrified me. It was what I felt through them. Something on the other side of their eyes. They could see it. I couldn't. *We* can't. Humans, I mean. Can't see what they see. So they showed me, I guess, their sense of it. Then, *bang*, all at once, morning came. Here I stood in my pajama bottoms, shivering, my toes covered in dew, these carcasses lying at my feet."

"That's awful," Annetta said.

Malik laughed a humorless, ironic bark. "That ain't all. It got weirder."

"How so?" I asked.

"This ain't easy to talk about. If anyone will believe me, it's you two, but it's still a struggle to say these things. I'm afraid of what happens after I do, you understand?"

I did. Speaking his experiences, sharing them, especially with me and Annetta, who'd believe him, made them real and closed the door on denying them, rationalizing them as a bad dream, forgetting. Giving that up didn't come easily.

"Yeah, I do," I said.

"So, I'm standing right here, barefoot and cold, with the sun coming over the horizon waking me up. I've lost hours of my life, can't account for that time at all, but there are dead critters at my feet, and as all of this rushes into my thoughts and my heart races, that damn black car rolls into my driveway."

Reflex snapped my gaze to the driveway, where only Annetta's Prius and Malik's Tundra sat. Then I stared into the Pine Barrens. The sense of something observing us, monitoring us overwhelmed me. I stepped closer to Annetta, protecting her and needing the reassurance of close contact.

"You remember the black car now?" Annetta said.

"Yes. They didn't want me to, not right away at least, but they changed their minds."

"Who changed their minds?" I said.

Malik looked at us, and I hated the confusion in his eyes, the pain of finding himself at such a desperate loss. "I don't... I don't know," he said. "The driver gave me a package and said not to open it until the three of us were together again. Got back in the car and drove away after that."

"What did the driver look like?" I said.

Malik shrugged. "Pale. No hair at all, like with alopecia. Dressed in black."

"Where's the package now?" Annetta said.

With a nod to the house, Malik said, "I left that inside. You think we should open it?"

CHAPTER NINETEEN

Staring at the package wrapped in plain brown paper, I wrestled to answer Malik's question. As far as we'd come this summer, nothing stopped us from calling it quits. Throw the package unopened into the trash. Burn it. Move on with our lives and hope none of the weirdness of the past few months moved on with us. Every next experience depended on us accepting the preceding one. We had walked through a door Patricia Sung had opened for us, through another opened by Malik, then the black car opened the next door, and we walked right through that one too. Now we stood on the threshold of a new one—and it felt different. No walking away after this. All the others had tested and measured us for the one door that led beyond the point of no return. Once we opened the package, we'd need to see things through to the end, wherever it led, and as that thought formed, I knew we'd do it. We had to do it. *I* had to. I didn't possess the will to turn away.

"If either of you want out," I said, "I'll open this on my own."

"Hell, no," Annetta said, "And let you have all the fun? We're in this together."

"Bigfoot threw a branch through my kitchen window, Ben. I'm not stopping until I get to the bottom of this insanity." Malik handed me a pair of scissors. "You can do the honors."

I poked the edge of one scissors blade under the wrapping and sliced it. Another few cuts and the paper fell away from a blue shoebox. No labels, no printing, only plain, blue cardboard. I set aside the scissors and lifted the lid. Crumpled newspaper lay inside and beneath it a manila envelope. I opened it, slid the contents onto Malik's kitchen table. Two file folders and a smaller envelope. I spread the folders and opened them. Each held an information sheet with a 3 x 5 portrait photo of a child paper-clipped to the top. One of a young Asian girl, maybe six or seven, with her dark hair in a ponytail. The other, a Caucasian boy, a bit older, eight or nine perhaps, square-jawed with wavy red hair, buzz-cut on the sides. The name on the girl's sheet read "Patty Sung." It listed an address in Calverton. The boy, apparently from Riverhead, was listed as "Jackie Kowaleski." Despite the difference decades made, I recognized their faces. Patricia Sung and her husband, Jack. Letterhead at the top of the information sheet read, "Camp Hero/ Project Vaudeville," the year typed beneath it: 1953.

The dossier for each child contained letters and reports from military scientists and doctors, forms for physicals given at six-month intervals, and time logs recording the dates on which they'd been "transported" to and from the research facility. A stamp in the upper left corner of each page read: *Top Secret*. Additional pictures clipped to the back of the folder showed the children sleeping in hospital-style beds, with electrodes fastened to their heads; receiving an injection; playing a game of Checkers with a woman in a lab coat—and, worst of all, strapped by their wrists to a metal chair in the center of a vast, empty room with utterly black walls. The last photo in each group showed an ordinary house. The house numbers in the image matched the address in the file.

I couldn't read any further through welling tears. Whether they came from sadness or fear, I couldn't say. I didn't know what to think, how to feel at the revelation that Malik's urban legend about experiments on kids contained more fact than fiction. Someone, or some*thing*, had dropped a secret hidden for decades in our lap and expected us to know what to do with it.

Reading over my shoulder, Malik said, "It's a prank, right? Conspiracy-theory nonsense. I bet someone is feeding us this to get it in the paper, drum up publicity for something."

"They sent three Bigfoots with some dead Montauk Monsters and a hairless man in a crazy black car to your out-of-the-way house for publicity?" Annetta said.

"Yeah, maybe they did. All of this could be fake," Malik said.

"You want publicity, you go on a talk show. You're deflecting," Annetta said.

"I'm not deflecting anything. You're out of your mind."

"Oh, I'm out of my mind? Really? Who bought a shark cage to trap Bigfoot?"

Their voices rose, ratcheting up the tension in the room. I closed the file folders and slapped my hand on the table. "Arguing won't help. Every step of the way, we've met this—whatever *this* is—head-on all summer, and we did it by sticking together. Don't let the mystery get under your skin now." I tapped the closed folders. "This is horrifying, and if it's true, having these papers in our possession probably puts us on the wrong side of half a dozen federal laws, yet here we are. This is evidence. Outside is more evidence. That's what we wanted, right? Physical proof of the Montauk Monster. That's a goodwill gesture from whoever is luring us down this path. They did us a favor. Now they want one in return."

"Which is what, exactly?" Annetta said.

I shrugged. "Uncover the real history at Camp Hero?"

"Some goodwill gesture," Malik said. "'Hey, we're doing this thing for you that you never asked us to do so you'll do this other thing for us.' That's manipulation."

Annetta said, "What if it's about Patricia and Jack? Maybe they want Patricia to stop interfering with Monty."

"They're not too concerned with Monty if they brought us three dead specimens."

Malik flopped onto one of the kitchen chairs. "Let's say you're right. What do we do? We can't find Ms. Sung and her husband to interview them. We have no other proof of Project Vaudeville. Would you report this story, Ben?"

Shaking my head, I said, "Not without corroboration or showing the documents to a forgery expert, and not without being able to account for how these papers came into our possession."

"Then we're back to square one," Annetta said.

"Maybe not."

I lifted the last envelope and opened it. It held a handful of Polaroid snapshots. Grainy and dark in many places, but clear enough for me to recognize the old radar antenna at Camp Hero and the couple at the center of the first photo.

Ethan, limping on crutches in his cast, a satchel slung across his torso. Lana, wearing a backpack. They stood on a path in Camp Hero Park. The second shot showed them farther along the trail, neither showing any awareness of being photographed. In the third, they'd stopped and stood looking at the ground in an overgrown area. The fourth showed Lana, crouching, gazing downward. Neither of them appeared in the fifth, a picture of what looked like an oversized manhole, the cover slid aside, the first three rungs of a ladder visible above a yawning darkness.

My head spun. The world turned elastic.

I dropped onto one of Malik's hardwood kitchen chairs for support, for a connection to tangible reality. My vision blurred. A moment, a few seconds, a few minutes of my life simply flickered out of existence, and then Annetta's voice, heavy with concern, called me back to my senses. Malik handed me a glass of water. The kitchen light hurt my eyes. I squinted. The roar of my pulse faded from my ears.

"Are you all right?" Annetta said, not the first time.

"Lightheaded, that's all," I said. "Those photos. I wasn't expecting… I don't know what I was expecting, but it wasn't that. That's why Ethan and Lana disappeared."

"They went down the rabbit hole," Malik said.

I weighed my next words carefully. The sense of standing on the edge of a strange and horrifying vista, of which I'd only glimpsed one tantalizing corner, set me thinking that all this from the start of summer until now — Ethan's car crash, Patricia Sung's twelve-legged spiders, Malik's Bigfoots, the Montauk Monster feeding frenzy, and maybe even my relationship with Annetta — had all been by design. As if an unseen influence played to our imaginations to send us down a narrow path of conjecture and experience to… what? To show us something incredible? Prepare us for this moment? Warn us? To stay away or to stay alert? To use us for an unknown goal? I didn't know. Nor could I articulate all that to Annetta and Malik right then. I wasn't sure I could describe how the fragments assembled in my brain. Instead, I said, "We have to go after them, find them. We can unravel everything, get all the answers. We can document every minute for the entire world to see. We have to go back to Camp Hero."

I had no idea then how both incredibly right and incredibly wrong I was.

CHAPTER TWENTY

It's fair at this point to question our judgment, our sanity, and our common sense, to cast a shady eye on everything I documented from that summer up to that moment, to stand back and shake your head at the three of us loading gear into Malik's Tundra for a second run at Camp Hero. Why not take the photos of Ethan and Lana to the police and ask them to search the park, the old buildings, and the tunnels beneath them? Or leave an anonymous tip? Or put everything we had on the Internet at once? Why not check ourselves into a hospital for psychiatric care? We thought of all those options while preparing that afternoon. Each one made sense in the normal world, where houses didn't disappear, monsters didn't vanish into underwater lights, and hairy, nine-foot-tall beasts didn't stalk ordinary homes on the edge of the Pine Barrens. We acted under the belief — no, the conviction — that we wouldn't ever have proof enough to support what we knew as true, at least not without seeing things through to the end.

We feared sending the police might close forever some unknown, undefined door through which Ethan and Lana might return. We felt tasked with a responsibility. Threatened by the aggressive nature of the Bigfoots, the stalking of the black car, the sense that as much as those Polaroids offered hope of finding my missing friends, they hinted at a dark, unthinkable fate for them if we refused to comply. Hostages to the mystery. So we filled the Tundra with flashlights and electric lanterns, ropes, food and water, Malik's Ketch-All poles and his tranquilizer pistol, a toolbox, my camera equipment, and anything else that might help. Annetta tucked the Montauk Monster hides into her satchel, and hell, if we thought Malik's kitchen sink might prove useful, we'd have pulled it out and thrown that in too.

We entered Camp Hero before dark, and then, after waiting for an opportunity to do so unseen, Malik drove his truck off the paved road and into the woods far enough to hide it with some dead branches pulled across the body. The position of the radar antennae in the Polaroids provided a general sense of the location of the trail down which Ethan and Lana had trod. With the antenna looming like a sinister mechanical eye in the spreading twilight, we loaded up with gear from the truck and then searched. After an hour, we found it, a narrow, overgrown dirt trail, and followed it to the end. A round, steel cover, roughly five feet in diameter. It capped a cement rim prodding up from the dirt. I pushed away the leaves and branches hiding it. The cover proved too heavy to move by hand. Malik retrieved a crowbar from his truck, and together we levered it up and slid it to the side, exposing a shaft in the ground. Cold, rotten air blew up from below. We scrunched our faces and waved our hands to disperse the odor.

Annetta switched on a flashlight and aimed the beam down. Ladder rungs mounted into the side of the shaft descended farther than the light's reach.

"We're doing this?" I said.

Malik nodded.

Annetta said, "We're doing it."

I clipped one of Malik's electric lanterns to my belt then lowered myself into the opening, finding the iron rung with my foot. I paused when my eyes met the cement rim. Above us, trees cut across the darkening sky as twilight gathered, and I thought maybe we should come back in the morning, do this by daylight, but then, with a glance into the dense black void beneath me, I couldn't see how day or night made a difference where we were going. I took the next two rungs, and the shaft enveloped me. Another rung. Another. I kept my pace steady, cautious, but afraid that if I stopped, I might lose the resolve to continue. Light flashed overhead. Annetta following me. Then Malik. None of us spoke, but the breath of our exertion echoed around us. I lost count of how many rungs I'd passed somewhere around forty-five or fifty. By the time I touched solid ground, the opening overhead looked like the moon, a circle of brightness in the night sky of a different world.

I switched on the Maglite Malik had given me. Tunnels branched off in three directions from the shaft's bottom. Ceiling fixtures in each tunnel suggested they'd once been brightly lit but looked as if they had gone dark forever ago. Annetta joined me at the bottom, then Malik, and we stared down each tunnel, daunted by the uncertainty.

"Tell you one thing," Malik said. "We ain't splitting up. That's for chumps. We stick together, don't let each other out of our sight. We on the same page?"

"Yeah, works for me," I said.

"Hell, yes, I'm not going off anywhere by myself," Annetta said.

"Good, so we'll take the tunnel to the right," Malik said. "When we had to clear a house, we always started to the right and worked our way around counterclockwise."

I aimed my light down that tunnel, took a step, breathed deeply, then entered.

Damp, moldy air enveloped me, so miasmic, I almost felt it pushing to either side of me and pooling around my legs, dragging at my feet. Beyond the spear of my flashlight beam, utter darkness held sway, the end of the tunnel invisible. We walked for what seemed like an hour but could have been only a few minutes before we arrived at a steel door. Time and rust held it stuck in place, but Malik and I shouldered it open, hinges squealing, metal grinding along the cement floor. A blast of warm air laden with a sour, milky odor billowed out. We recoiled and covered our faces until the worst of the stink dissipated.

In the room beyond, two industrial-style desks, side by side, faced the entrance, a wall of filing cabinets behind them. An office sofa sat against the wall to the right of the door. Two other doors, opposite each other, broke the remaining walls. We checked the desks, then the filing cabinets, opening each drawer carefully, spilling light into empty containers lined with dust and scraps of paper. Faded labels on the filing cabinets showed a year and a letter range, "1948, A-C," "1948, D-I," and so on, the order beginning again with each year, up through 1963, leaving the last two drawers of the cabinets unlabeled. I tucked my flashlight under my arm, uncased my camera, and took pictures of everything, even the empty drawers, and the desks.

Annetta opened the door on the right of the room. Another office, an abandoned desk and chair. More filing cabinets. More emptiness, dust, and nothing, but the hint of something that had been, or might have been, echoes of a distant past almost too secret even to have been forgotten. I snapped more pictures, recorded it all as best I could. Silence muted our footsteps, and my skin bristled with anxiety, a sense of trespassing, of risk.

Behind the second door, we found a large room that confirmed our worst fears. A dozen steel-frame beds like the ones pictured in the photos of Patricia and Jack lined the walls, six to a side, and a large table and chairs waited at the far end of the room. Bare of mattresses, pillows, and blankets, the beds resembled archaic torture devices. A flash of red caught my eye. I knelt for a closer look and found a single, red checker wedged between the wall and the leg of one of the beds. I showed it to Annetta and Malik, then slid it into my pocket. I took more pictures. We found nothing more of interest. For all we knew, these rooms had served as an infirmary, though we couldn't explain why anyone would locate an infirmary underground at the bottom of a long ladder. Without proof, it didn't matter, and any proof that had once been here had long ago been removed, boxed up, filed away in some anonymous military archive—or fed to an incinerator, maybe. Erased.

We backtracked to our starting point and took the second tunnel. This one, much shorter than the first, led to an open, steel pocket door and into a cavernous black room. Walls, ceiling, and floor, all a dull, matte black. A room from the pictures. Patty in one, Jack in the other, taking their turns sitting at the center of the space, alone, surrounded by black, staring into nothingness, or something beyond the nothingness. Unlike the rest of the place, the black room had no odor, as if it had been sterilized. A disquiet hung about it. The resonance of terrible things done long ago that had never truly ended. The feeling of invisible doors waiting to open all around us. The room's strange paint absorbed the light from my flash, making it difficult to get clear shots.

The last corridor sloped downward and proved the longest. It curved in places, and near the end, made a sharp right. A faint, shimmering emerald glow came from around the corner, hazy in the dusty air. We approached with caution, hugging the wall, lights aimed down to show the path. After several deep breaths, I stepped around the corner. The floor declined toward a broad opening, from which the glow emanated. Annetta touched my shoulder. I glanced at her, too anxious to speak, her message clear. *Be careful.* I nodded, then led us down the slope and into an expansive room filled with green illumination. A river of it ran from one wall to the next, a span of 150 or 200 feet. With no visible source or outlet, the rippling green vibrancy appeared to emerge directly from one wall and vanish into the other. It flowed and twined like currents in a river. Through it swam a steady parade of Montauk Monsters. Hundreds of them, passing by us, crossing the distance in seconds. A thousand must have gone by in the time we stood, stunned, staring at the inexplicable sight.

The room vibrated with a deep hum. Malik nudged me, pointed at my forgotten camera. I lifted it to my eye and took pictures. I walked the length of the stream, ducked down, and crossed under it, to take pictures from the other side. All the while, Montauk Monsters swam by us from one wall to the next. As I studied the phenomena and my eyes adjusted, my perception caught up with my senses. The light and its occupants didn't so much flow across the room as they were visible from the room, as if a giant scalpel had sliced an incision in the air and peeled back the flap, providing a glimpse beneath the skin of our reality. And whenever you cut flesh, it bled.

A parallel world bleeding into ours. Did ours bleed into it?

Beyond the Monsters, a dark shape writhed, deep black in the green, a thing of lashing appendages and an enormous, bulbous body. It rolled and floated, churning the green, scattering Monsters ahead of it, gliding, growing larger, nearer, and the tip of one of its flicking, whip-like limbs aimed at me, reaching, grasping, an invisible projection tickling my brain. The very tip of it, mottled green-and-black, prodded out, stretching the light stream like a membrane, unable to break through it, but reaching toward my forehead, my body frozen in place—then a scream, not my voice, another's, though I couldn't tell if it came from Annetta or Malik, or if it even occurred in the present or simply spilled over from the past, dizzying me, breaking the spell.

I folded to my knees. The appendage withdrew. The black creature lingered, a leviathan hanging over my head in the green light. Annetta and Malik whispered in my ears—no, shouted in them, but only a whisper of their voices reached me, and then I rose to my feet, shuffling out of the room with their aid and up the slope where all three of us collapsed on the floor.

We sat and stared at each other, too shocked to speak.

Then a voice from the dark said, "You shouldn't be here."

All three of us jumped and screamed.

CHAPTER TWENTY-ONE

A child glowed in the tunnel. Two young Montauk Monsters perched on her shoulders. She wore a little girl's frilly Minnie Mouse nightgown, her feet bare. She smiled, narrowing her eyes, her teeth gleaming white in the dark. With her black hair and ponytail, I recognized her.

"Patricia?" I said. "Ms. Sung?"

She giggled. "You're silly." One of the Monsters scrambled down her body, sat at her feet, and glared at me. "Do you work with the doctors?"

"No," I said. "We're visitors."

"No, you're not," little Patricia said. "Visitors aren't allowed."

"Are you all right, kid? Are you hurt?" Malik clambered upright and approached the girl, only to recoil when the Monster by her feet reared up and snapped its beak at him. The second leapt at him from her shoulder, landing on the ground and joining in the show of force.

"Don't touch me," Patricia said.

"Okay, okay, I won't touch you. None of us is going to touch you. We want to help," he said, backing away.

"I know that," the girl said. "You can't touch me, though, because if you do, you have to come with me."

"Come with you where?" Annetta said.

"Into the green light, to the warm fuzzy place, where my friends live," she said.

"The light in the other room?" Annetta said.

"Uh-huh," Patricia said. "It's a bad time to go. The prickly ball is too close."

"What's the prickly ball?" Malik asked.

"You saw it." Patricia pointed at me. "It tried to touch him."

"What would've happened if it touched me?" I asked.

"Then you'd have to go with it, into the green light."

"Did you come out of the green light?" Annetta asked.

Patricia smiled again as one of the Monsters scampered up her side, back to its perch by her neck. "Hey, maybe you guys can take me home? Can you give me a ride when you leave?"

"I don't know," I said. "What would your doctors say?"

Wrinkling her face, Patricia said, "I don't like *them.* I sneak out all the time. They never know."

"Are they here too?" Malik said.

"Not now, no, just me. I snuck out."

Annetta approached Patricia and knelt eye level with her, careful not to make contact. "You're all alone?"

"I have my friends." Patricia stroked the fur of the Monster on her shoulder. The other one curled around and scrambled up to her other shoulder, seeking its share of the attention. "These two are kids, like me, but the grown-up ones are my friends too. They show me how to move through the green light and how to come back here."

I backed up to the turn in the corridor and stared at the green glow from the bottom of the slope. More questions than I could count flashed to mind. Obvious ones, such as what the hell the green light meant and what did it show us, to odd and mundane ones, like, was Patricia cold walking around this place in a nightshirt and no shoes. I found it impossible to answer even the simple ones. Instead, I fell back on what I knew and lifted my camera. I snapped pictures of Patricia, who mugged for the lens. Her glow appeared richer and more shimmery on the screen. It glistened with colors like the fur of the Montauk Monsters and Bigfoots. Looking at it long enough, I saw patterns in the coruscations, a rhythm to the colors.

"Have you seen any other people here recently?" I asked.

"I see people here all the time. Sometimes all the doctors and the nurses. Some days the soldiers come. Other days, they're all gone, and I'm by myself, except when other people come. The hat man comes a lot when no one else is here."

"Who's the hat man?" I asked.

Patricia shrugged. "He wears all black. His hat is black too. I don't like him. I hide when he comes."

I dug the Polaroids of Ethan and Lana out of my satchel and showed them to Patricia by flashlight. "Did you see this man and woman?"

She stared at the picture, then nodded, her face serious and sad. "Uh-huh."

"Did you talk to them?"

"I didn't like them. They scared me. I hid in the black room."

"They didn't come in there and find you?"

"They came in, but I hid in the black, outside the walls. They couldn't ever find me there. Only Jackie ever found me there. I'm the best at hide and seek."

"Did they leave then?"

"No."

"But they did leave?"

"No."

Annetta took my hand in hers, squeezed it.

"What happened to them?"

"The hat man took them into the green," she said.

"How... is that possible?"

Patricia shrugged. "It just is."

"Can we get them back from the green light?"

Whatever the answer, it frightened me. Either Ethan and Lana were lost forever, or I was obligated to rescue them from something I hadn't yet begun to understand. But I never heard Patricia's reply. A mighty rumble shuddered along the tunnel, quaking the underground facility so much that dust and bits of cement rained from the ceiling. The green light flared. Patricia squealed out, "The prickly ball!" and then fled up the tunnel.

I chased her, terrified she might get hurt, or we might lose her, or we might lose our key to unlocking the mysteries that surrounded us. I caught up in time to watch her run down the tunnel to the black room and slip inside the door. I followed, swinging my flashlight beam to every part of the room, exposing nothing but dark surfaces that seemed to drink the light—and then for an immeasurably small flicker of time, I saw Patricia, not as the little girl with Montauk Monsters for pets, but grown-up, elderly, as I had first met her. She stepped into an opening in the black wall, a sliver of light filled with bright green grass and trees, crystal blue skies, and the house where Annetta and I had visited her. Jack stood on the front porch, a can of Coors in hand. All this I viewed so fast and fleeting it burned an impression in my brain more than I actually saw it. Then the sliver closed, and the room returned to black.

Malik and Annetta called to me from the door. I ignored them, thoughts racing to unlock the secret of where Patricia had come from, where she'd gone. Finding nothing but blank, black walls, I touched one. Cold, gritty, solid. No way in, out, or through it.

Malik and Annetta grabbed my arms then and dragged me from the room. Everything shook. The ground rolled. They led me back to where we'd started, to the bottom of the ladder, the dying moon of light at its pinnacle urging me to climb. I refused. Down the left tunnel, green light pulsed. It flowed like water. Montauk Monsters scurried and swam in it. Behind them, the shadow of the dark ball rippled. Its giant cilia wriggled ahead of it, all of them freed from the light stream. I knew then why we'd been shown the things we'd seen that summer, why we stood here in dark tunnels burdened by enigma. What purpose we'd been given.

"We can't go," I said. "We have to make sure that thing doesn't get out of here."

CHAPTER TWENTY-TWO

Green light rose, submerging the tunnel in its languid depth. The sight of it defied easy perception. Imagine looking through a window with the infinite, looping structure of a Mobius strip, seeing slivers of the world, the window not only moving but rotating, things gliding through it, half-exiting in one place before half-reappearing in another. A dizzying, headache-inducing roller coaster ride during which your feet never leave solid ground. Then, as the light intensified, sounds came. The chittering of more than a thousand Montauk Monsters swimming in the green, an enormous school of them. The thrum of waves beating a sandy beach. A soul-trembling grumble from the prickly ball. Annetta and Malik tugged on my arms and pled with me to hurry up the ladder. A smell filled the tunnels. Reminiscent of the repugnant odor that surrounded the Bigfoots, but not as intense or as foul. My hair rose on end as if the air held a massive charge of static electricity.

A Montauk Monster poked out of the green and dropped to the tunnel floor. Its exit left a hole in the air through which green wisps of haze trailed out. Two more Monsters followed, then the trio rushed at us, flashing their beaks, snapping their teeth as if to attack us, but before they reached us, they cut left and raced down the tunnel to the Black Room. Something else poked through the hole in the air they created, not a Montauk Monster but the tip of one of the prickly ball's feelers. It slid through and lashed until it struck the ceiling of the tunnel. As if alerted by the contact, the prickly ball wriggled and brushed a dozen of its cilia to herd part of the school toward the hole. The current created by its feelers sent little herds of Montauk Monsters through the green, rending a larger opening in the air. Green mist plumed out. The prickly ball pressed against the cut, forcing feelers and part of its scaly mass through, exerting itself to widen the opening, but somehow it lacked the strength to budge it even an inch. Whatever contained it held tight, though the Monsters could break through.

"It needs the Monties to get out," I said.

Annetta let go of my arm. "What are you talking about?"

I pointed to more Monsters, falling to the floor, trailing curls of green fog, then joining the wriggling line of them rushing away to the Black Room. Prickly ball sent a feeler out the hole, right after them.

"See? It waits for them to breach whatever's holding back the green, then tries to come through itself. The prickly ball wants to come into our world, but it can't on its own."

"I think he's right," Malik said.

"How does that help us? Why are we not getting the hell out of here?" Annetta said.

"What if it *does* come through?" I said.

"I don't want to stick around to find out," she said.

"Exactly. It's going to be bad. So we can't let it happen," I said. "That's what all this has been about. Why the three of *us* were chosen, I don't know, but we were. Patricia Sung reached out to you, Annetta. She knew this was coming and needed someone who'd pay attention. The Bigfoots picked you for the same reason, Malik. Whatever they knew about you two told them you'd be receptive and would see this through."

"And you, Ben? You weren't chosen. You're here by chance," Annetta said.

"Am I, though? Ethan crashed when a black sedan ran him off the road. Otherwise, he'd be here instead of me. But maybe they changed their mind and took him out of the mix. They wanted *me* here instead of *him*. Except he didn't leave well enough alone. He and Lana stuck their noses in anyway, came here, found this, and… I don't know."

I had no idea what had happened to them. Maybe they'd gone into the green light, as Patty said. A horrifying prospect. Or they'd gotten so frightened by what they learned they went into hiding. Or the photos were faked, and they'd never come here. Or they were part of the hidden hand that guided our path, and when they'd fulfilled their purpose, they simply vanished. Or they'd given all this up, flown to Vegas to get married and start a new life. Who knew? Not me. Not anyone, as far as I could tell, except for Ethan and Lana themselves. If nothing else, the fact that we didn't know so much—*couldn't* know it, could only guess at, sense, or assume the truth — defined everything we'd experienced this summer.

On the surface, it appeared our world intersected with another. Some creatures could pass through the barrier; others couldn't; and that a hairless man in a strange black car patrolled the border with the help of Bigfoots. That sounded bat-guano loco. For all I knew, it described only the picture as they wanted me to see it, not reality at all. Then Malik asked the obvious question.

"Who the hell are *they*, Ben? Who do you think is out there pulling our strings?" he said. "I can tell you from hard-earned experience it's easy to see patterns where none exist, tempting to assign motives to things that happened by chance. We have no evidence to prove your theory."

No answer came to mind. I watched the churning green. It had shrunk, retreated a few feet. I guessed that losing so many Montauk Monsters had stalled its advance.

"That's not accurate, Malik." Annetta stepped between Malik and me. In her arms curled a Montauk Monster, its fur shimmering with an oil slick rainbow of color, green haze around its eyes. "We have the evidence right here."

Chapter Twenty-Three

"It says we have to lead the prickly ball to the Blackout Room to stop it," Annetta said.

"The rodent told you that?" Malik said.

"It's not a rodent. It's... not something that fits any of our zoological classifications. But, yes, it told me that. It said Patty called us friends, so it's asking for help. The Monties don't want to let the prickly ball through. They know it doesn't belong in our world, that *they* don't belong in our world, but they like it here, so they come through sometimes but never stay. If the prickly ball comes through, it'll be trapped. It can't pass through on its own like them because it doesn't have fur. Something about their fur lets them slip between worlds, but the prickly ball's scales don't work like that."

"Gimme a break. I didn't hear a word from that damn thing," Malik said.

"You have to touch it," Annetta said.

"Say what?" Malik said.

"Touch its fur. Go ahead. It said it's okay." Annetta smiled. "It promises it won't bite."

Taking a deep breath, I stroked the Monster's fur. It tingled against my hand but felt soft and thick beneath the energy. Malik did the same. Color filled my eyes for half a second, searing bright, a flash full of so many hues, some I couldn't name, some I'd never seen, others familiar yet richer, more saturated than I knew they could be. Then the colors vanished, leaving me blind while my eyes adjusted again to the gloom. Everything Annetta had told us the Monster had said was true. Malik knew it too. We lowered our hands, no doubt left in our minds.

"How do we lure that thing into the Blackout Room?" I said.

Annetta approached the green, raised the Monty to it, and let it jump back into the stream. "We use the hides and follow this little guy's lead."

She retrieved the Monty furs from her satchel and handed one to each of us. We held them and waited. Seconds passed. Nothing happened. A shadow appeared in the light. Another prickly ball, I thought at first, and my heart skipped a beat, but then it scattered into smaller shadows formed by clusters of Monties.

They swam what seemed like toward us in the distorted view we had of their world, then the first group broke through, ripping open a new hole in the green. Prickly ball sent feelers right after them.

The panicked Monties scrambled in circles until Annetta snatched one up, held it for a moment, then all of them fell into line and followed her as she raced down the tunnel to the Blackout Room. The green light stretched and flowed after them, tracing their wake, tethered by the wisps of emerald haze trailing from their fur. Another group burst through. I grabbed one, held it, and then rushed down the tunnel. All the others and the light stream followed, the prickly ball lashing its feelers through the openings. A third group came. Malik followed our example and lifted one to his arms. Then another group came, then another, and another, and each time one of us plucked a single Monty from the huddle and carried it down the tunnel, directing the light stream to the Blackout Room. The rent in the green grew larger with every group, and more of the prickly ball bulged through. I flashed back to a junior high school health class diagram of a hernia, and the thought — so utterly incongruous and unexpected, yet so completely accurate as an analogy — started me laughing. By their looks, Annetta and Malik must've thought I'd snapped.

Then the Monties stopped. The prickly ball swelled through the openings in the green, pushed against the tunnel walls and ceiling, trying to ooze its scaly mass into our world. We couldn't let it emerge outside the Blackout Room. From what the Monties had told us, releasing it anywhere else would set it free in our world.

I wrapped the Monty hide around my hand and reached into the green light.

Even through the hide, the energy of another world lit up my nerves like a Christmas tree overloaded with twinkling lights. Monties swarmed my hand. Thousands rushed me, rioting, spilling out all over the green, releasing more of the prickly ball. Following my example,

Annetta and Malik wrapped the hides around their hands and guided the Monties toward me. Another huge group came, following my hide. I swept them the length of the tunnel, out of the green, and into the Blackout Room, tearing the widest gash yet in the light—and the prickly ball followed.

I dashed to the center of the Black Room. When the prickly ball's last tendril slithered through the doorway, a rush of energy blew past me and slammed the door shut.

Cut off from Annetta and Malik, cold flowed into me, into my bones. The door, also painted dead black, undetectable from within the room while closed, had severed the head of the light stream, leaving me stuck in the dark with the prickly ball, bursting through the tattered remnants of the green light in a dozen different places. More Monties broke through. I didn't need to guide them now. They simply fell into the room, scurried into the dark, and vanished. None of those we'd led here so far remained, as if they'd all slipped through slivers of space in the walls, like the one through which Patricia had exited. I wanted them to stop. We'd succeeded in bringing the prickly ball to the Blackout Room, but the Monties kept coming, eating away at the green until I realized, inevitably, the beast would enter our world entirely.

The room rumbled. Everything vibrated. All around me, the black shimmered. Pressure in the air changed abruptly, and my ears popped. The green flickered out, gone, leaving me no more than ten yards from the prickly ball, a scaly, slime-coated, pulsing mass, bristling with feelers that raised it off the floor, feelers that stretched in all directions to assess its surroundings, feelers that, when they reached me, stopped inches from contact and sprouted eyes that glowed like miniature suns and spoke of the power within the beast.

I should've been terrified in that moment. Instead, my senses sharpened. Everything around me ground to a flicker-frame, slow-motion experience. It overwhelmed me. I couldn't form a coherent thought in response, only absorb everything I saw, heard, smelled, even tasted on the air rushing into my mouth, and felt against my skin, the tickle of invisible touches from something unknown. Then a sliver opened in the black, in the floor beneath the prickly ball. A sliver that widened to a gawping slice of blue light, through which—for the moment I looked—an indigo world of stone and lightning showed before enormous black, trident-tipped arms rose, digging the points of their pincers into the substance of the prickly ball. Four of them appeared and bit into it. They dragged it down, ripping its feelers off the walls, off the floor and ceiling, dragging its burning eyes from me. A squeal of pain, frustration, defeat, and anger pierced the room, though even in the moment, I wondered if I were imprinting on that sound human emotions meaningless to the thing that made it. Then the ball vanished into the crevasse, which snapped shut, and a *whoosh* of air blasted across the room as the pressure changed once again.

I crashed to the floor in utter darkness.

The door creaked and swung open. Flashlight beams poked through.

Footsteps. Familiar hands.

Annetta and Malik helped me to my feet. Guided me to the ladder.

We ascended. Somehow, I made the climb. My memory of leaving that place exists in sensory scraps that end with fresh air, trees, and a star-filled night sky, and Annetta pressing a cloth to my head as she said, "Oh my god, he's bleeding from his ears."

Chapter Twenty-Five

The day after our night underground, a doctor told me my eardrums had burst but would heal. That came as a relief. Though the world sounded muffled and far away for me until they did, it seemed an appropriate aftereffect for an experience that had all but removed me from the world in which I'd once lived. No going back after all that, right? Annetta, Malik, and I agreed on that, though we differed on what to do next.

Malik declared it all done and over. Message received. Mission accomplished. He lost all interest in any chance of a big story or trapping a Bigfoot on his property. When we returned to his house the morning after, he eyed the Pine Barrens with suspicion and hurried us inside. To this day, I don't think he's set foot in those woods again. Last I visited, he moved his grill around front and liked to do his outdoor living off the front porch, with the house squarely between him and the Barrens. Janae came back. She asked us very few questions and accepted our assurances that if any more weirdness came around, we'd leave Malik out of it.

Annetta and I were more simpatico. We wanted to know more.

For a month after the night at Camp Hero, nothing happened to us except ordinary life. She resumed teaching, and I drummed up a few freelance gigs, and as things settled, she broke her lease in Brooklyn and moved in with me. We organized our notes, filed the videos and photos, recorded all the locations, dates, and times, and created a comprehensive record of the whole thing. Perfect and complete except for the one thing needed to make anyone other than us accept it as fact—evidence.

Annetta had tried to hold onto a Monty that night, but they'd slipped through her hands as if greased or semi-immaterial, she told me. The hides we used dissolved after we exposed them to the green light. The carcasses, left at Malik's, were gone when we returned, dragged away by scavengers, reclaimed by Bigfoot, or simply dissipated into thin air, faded back from where they'd come. We made a few excursions out east to search for Ms. Sung's place, but after the first failed attempt, those became more about walking the beach and stocking up at farm stands than finding that elusive house and its inhabitants.

Some nights we talked through the story, turned it over in new directions, asked again questions we'd pondered for months in hopes of uncovering a new answer, but as time passed, more and more of our nights turned to simply enjoying each other's company.

Around Thanksgiving, a letter addressed to me came in the mail with no return address.

Inside the envelope, a single-sheet, typewritten note from Ethan. It read:

> *Dear Ben,*
> *Apologize for leaving so suddenly and no goodbyes. Life turns in funny directions.*
>
> *Good you did what needed doing. The story is yours.*
> *Lana and I are fine and well. Miss you.*
>
> *Hope to see you again.*
>
> *Sincerely, Your Friend,*
> *Ethan*

I took no reassurance from the note. The stilted language hinted that the Ethan I knew hadn't written it. Either someone sent it to me in hopes of stopping me from looking for him and Lana, or Ethan had so changed as to render him incapable of writing the way he once did. Annetta agreed. All we took from it was the possibility that Ethan and Lana remained somewhere in the world, and we might find them one day. Even that felt like a stretch. We added the letter to the file and stopped mentioning it by Christmas.

We flew down to Florida to spend the holidays with my parents. When we returned home, we found a Christmas card from Malik in the mail. A brief note scrawled below the holiday message: "All quiet here and thank God for that."

A new year came, and life went on. It might seem strange to anyone reading this that we could fall back into the normality of routine, return to the grind as if any of those mundane things that fill most people's days — fill *our* days — mattered. We took comfort in it. We knew things almost no one else knew or would ever know, and we didn't abandon them. We kept our eyes and ears open. We watched the news and lurked on forums like the one Ethan and Lana had run. Once I saw that black car glide by down a side street and out of sight before I could react. Every day, all day, I felt watched. Both of us did. We lived with a sense of boundary, that if we picked up our investigation again, resumed our search for answers, came too close to evidence of any kind, something would step into our path and interfere, maybe with our lives, maybe much more. We lived with a constant vague sense of threat. And so we would've continued if not for a voicemail from Malik that came that spring.

He didn't speak at first. I heard only crickets and wind. Then the unmistakable *thunk* of wood against wood, followed by a single howl. Then Malik's voice: "I can't go through this again, Ben, but I thought you should know. I hope you and Annetta are doing well. I'm sorry for dropping this in your lap." In the background, more knocking came. "Stay safe, my friend." The message ended.

I shared it with Annetta. We added it to the file, and for a week, tried to ignore it, forget about it, just one more piece no one would believe. Then I found the spider. Twelve legs, the extra ones tipped with three-pronged pincers. Purple light shimmered in its many eyes. It lingered long enough for me to spot it in the corner above my desk, and then it scurried into a nearby shadow and never came out. That represented so much we'd experienced, so much we'd questioned about creatures that scuttled in and out of reality. Chromatic-furred beasts. Twelve-legged spiders small enough to hold with a pin or large enough to crack through space and time and drag a monster into unknown depths. It all came down to perspective and relativity, my twelve-legged spider theory of existence. Was that spider's gentle presence meant as a warning? A summons? Was it only a random sighting? Neither Annetta nor I knew. We took only one thing from its presence. No matter what we did, if we pretended we had no interest in revisiting the past and stirring up old mysteries or dove back in with all our hearts, we'd never live free and unwatched again.

AFTERWORD

My meetings with Ben Keep occurred in the late spring of the year following these events. Ben seemed haunted, resigned, determined, and vaguely angry. He shared all his recordings, photos, notes, and files. I drew upon them liberally to create this narrative, although they alone provide insufficient evidence to prove his story. All of them could have been digitally altered or generated. Some are less clear than Ben took them to be, but then he experienced everything they captured. I did not. Per his instructions, these documents are secured. He asked me to keep them safe and not share them with anyone until I received word from him that it was safe to do so.

The one exception he allowed was for me to play samples for my publisher as needed to convince them this story needed telling. For though Ben never said it directly, I believe that was his purpose in asking me to write this account. He believes the world is not ready to accept the events described here as true, and that it must be prepared to do so, familiarized with pieces of a large puzzle that might one day be completed and revealed.

Where Ben and Annetta went after our last meeting, I don't know.

I've driven by their house several times. It stands unoccupied, dark at night, and still by day. I stopped going there, though, stopped any attempt to keep tabs on Ben because the last time I drove by it, a black car — the make and model of which I had never seen — sat down the block with old-fashioned gold-on-black license plates and tinted windows all around, and I felt an undeniable sense of being watched.

Make of this what you will. I plan, like Malik, to move on with my life. My obligation to Ben fulfilled, my interest in these strange occurrences concluded.

— James Chambers
Northport, NY

ABOUT THE AUTHOR

James Chambers is an award-winning author of horror, crime, fantasy, and science fiction. He wrote the Bram Stoker Award®-winning graphic novel, *Kolchak the Night Stalker: The Forgotten Lore of Edgar Allan Poe*. *Publisher's Weekly* described *The Engines of Sacrifice*, his collection of four Lovecraftian-inspired novellas published by Dark Regions Press as "…chillingly evocative…" in a starred review. Booklist described his collection, *On the Night Border*, as "a haunting exploration of the space where the real world and nightmares collide."

He has authored the short story collection *Resurrection House* and several novellas, including *The Dead Bear Witness* and *Tears of Blood*, in the Corpse Fauna novella series. He also wrote the illustrated story collection, *The Midnight Hour: Saint Lawn Hill and Other Tales*, created in collaboration with artist Jason Whitley.

His short stories have appeared in dozens of anthologies and other publications. He edited the anthology, *Under Twin Suns: Alternate Histories of the Yellow Sign*, and co-edited *A New York State of Fright: Horror Stories from the Empire State*.

He has also written numerous comic books including *Leonard Nimoy's Primortals*, the critically acclaimed "The Revenant" in *Shadow House*, *The Midnight Hour* with Jason Whitley.

He lives in New York.

Visit his website: www.jameschambersonline.com.

ABOUT THE ARTIST

Although Jason Whitley has worn many creative hats, he is at heart a traditional illustrator and painter. With author James Chambers, Jason collaborates and illustrates the sometimes-prose, sometimes graphic novel, *The Midnight Hour*, which is being collected into one volume by eSpec Books. His and Scott Eckelaert's newspaper comic strip, Sea Urchins, has been collected into four volumes. Along with eSpec Books' Systema Paradoxa series, Jason is working on a crime noir graphic novel. His portrait of Charlotte Hawkins Brown is on display in the Charlotte Hawkins Brown Museum.

artist's rendition of a Montauk Monster

MONTAUK MONSTER

(Also known as Monty.)

ORIGINS: Theories abound about this creature, ranging from the proposition that it is a hoax, to claims it is a mutant product of scientific experimentation. The most common belief is that the discovery was nothing more than a decomposing mammal whose remains were distorted by prolonged submersion in sea water. Some believe that the truth has been covered up in a conspiracy of lies. As the only evidence is photographic, all theories remain speculation.

DESCRIPTION: While primarily representing as mammalian, the Montauk Monster is distinguished by a beaked upper jaw, with pointed teeth along the lower. Other features include fur, a long tail, and flat paws tipped with nail-like claws.

LIFE CYCLE: Unknown.

HISTORY: The original remains were discovered in 2008 by three girls walking along the Ditch Plain Beach. The girls photographed the creature, but before anyone could be called in to identify the animal, another individual proportedly removed the remains to a friend's property, with the intention of give the bones to a local artist to be included in an exhibition. When approached for confirmation, the gentleman in question reported that someone had stolen the body.

Despite significant media interest, most parties involved remain closed-mouthed, leading to the speculation that the the hoax or conspiracy theories may not be far from the mark.

It is believed by some that the creature was an escaped mutant from the nearby Plum Island laboratory, which studies animal disease.

Yet others claim the corpse is nothing more than a racoon, pitbull, coyote, or de-shelled turtle, though there are reasons each of these classifications is not perfectly matched with the evidence.

After the 2008 discovery, there have been multiple discoveries of Montauk Monster remains worldwide, but no definitive identification as no living specimen has been observed.

artist's rendition of a Bigfoot

BIGFOOT

(Also known as Sasquatch, Yeti, Skunk Ape, and various other names worldwide.)

ORIGINS: These creatures are theorized to be descended from *Gigantopithecus*, a prehistoric ape once found on the Asian continent.

Accounts have been documented all over North America and worldwide, though a large percentage of sightings come from the Pacific Northwest.

DESCRIPTION: Bigfoot is a classification, with individual species names and descriptions varying by region.

They are hirsute humanoids ranging in height from six to ten feet tall, with fur ranging from white to reddish brown to black, depending on region. Their characteristic big feet can range from one to two feet long and are said to be about one third wider than the typical human foot. Primarily, prints have been said to have five toes, but there have been claims of prints found with anywhere from two to six toes, occasionally including claws. Facial features are similar to great apes, with large eyes, prominent brows, and large, low forehead. The head is characterized by a crest and is rounded.

LIFE CYCLE: Unknown. However, some witness testimony cites that these creatures live in family groups similar to apes.

HISTORY: Native American tribes have long had legends about bigfoot type creatures, documented by cave paintings depicting them, but the earliest written account was in 1811. David Thompson encountered the Spokanes while mapping the wilds of Canada and North America. This tribe shared tales of hairy giants in the mountains that stole both salmon and people, on occasion. This account was the first mention of the infamous footprints.

In support of these accounts, a miner named Albert Ostman shared many decades later how he was carried off in his sleep in 1924 by a family of Sasquatch, which is behavior seen in modern apes as well.

Also in 1924, in the region of Mt. St. Helens, a group of prospectors had an encounter with a group of bigfoots that turned rather violent. After one of their party fired on a solitary creature earlier in the day, the party found themselves beseiged that night, with multiple bigfoots roaring in the night and casting big rocks against the walls of the prospectors' sturdy log cabin.

In the morning, the men went to sneak away, only to encounter a lone bigfoot, which they shot, but no remains were ever recovered.

The most famous encounter, however, took place in 1967 when the legendary Patterson-Gimlin Film was captured near Orleans, California. There has been heated debate as to the film's authenticity, with analysis presented both supporting and refuting the claims of an actual encounter.

The scientific argument against the existence of bigfoots is the resources needed to sustain a viable popluation to maintain a species of that size, in the region where the sightings have been documented. However, there is a faction among the scientific community that feels there is sufficient evidence to warrant further investigation.

CAPTURE THE CRYPTIDS!

Cryptid Crate is a monthly subscription box filled with various cryptozoology and paranormal themed items to wear, display and collect. Expect a carefully curated box filled with creeptastic pieces from indie makers and artisans pertaining to bigfoot, sasquatch, UFOs, ghosts, and other cryptid and mysterious creatures (apparel, decor, media, etc).

http://CryptidCrate.com

CPSIA information can be obtained
at www.ICGtesting.com
Printed in the USA
JSHW020917290521
15281JS00002B/9

9 781949 691597